sweet sixteen

Published by Silver Sky Publishing Inc.

Cover Designer
Regina Wamba, Mae I Design
www.maeidesign.com

Editor
Lisa Hollett, Silently Correcting Your Grammar

Copy Editor
Taylor Bellitto

Interior Design and Formatting
Christine Borgford, Type A Formatting
www.typeAformatting.com

sweet sixteen

BRENDA ROTHERT

one

Gin

I DON'T BELONG HERE.

The thought occurs to me for at least the thousandth time as I walk down a crowded hallway at Roper High School after my last class of the day. I'm behind a couple of sophomore girls who apparently just left geography class.

"I don't get it," one of them says to the other. "Why is it called South America if it's not even, like, *America*? America is America."

"Right?" The other one nods as she scrolls through her smartphone.

"It's like toilet paper. Why do they call it that when it's not really paper?"

"It's really dumb," her friend agrees.

And this is what I'm up against in my small-town high school—girls who think the word *plutocracy* somehow refers to their favorite Disney character.

Though I've lived in Roper my whole life, I've never felt

completely at home. There are labels for everyone here—jock, slut, nerd, freak . . . and so many others. None of them really applies to me, though.

I do get called a freak sometimes since I started coloring my red hair black, and sometimes I'm labeled a lesbian for not batting my eyelashes at football players. I'm not gay, but I feel no urge to set the record straight. Who cares what the assholes at this school think anyway? I'm out of here in nine months.

And when I say out of here, I mean Roper High School will just be a distant memory for me. I'm going to NYU, and while I might come back home on occasion to visit my mom, I won't be catching up with people I went to school with. No class reunions for this girl. Won't be liking people's drunken Facebook photos, either.

It's going to be *peace out*, Roper High.

"Hey." My friend Lauren falls into step beside me.

"Hey."

"You going to play practice?" she asks me.

"Yeah."

I'll keep in touch with Lauren, and our friend Raj, after high school. Like me, they don't agonize over which piece of Roper High spirit wear to put on every Friday for football game day. The rest of this place lives and breathes football, while the three of us live and breathe seeing the rest of the world as soon as we graduate.

I reach my locker, and Lauren leans up against the one next to it as I open mine and empty my books onto the shelf. She looks at the chipped blue nail polish on the stubby nails she bites when she's bored.

"This was the longest day ever," she says. "And I have to work from five to eight tonight. Woo-fucking-hoo."

I smile at her deadpan tone. Lauren and I have been friends since she moved here in third grade. We bonded over both having unfortunate names. With dirty blond hair that hangs in her eyes, thick, black eyeliner, and a lip ring, she's about as un-*Lauren* as it gets.

And my mom, though she has a very dark, creative mind she calls on to write horror novels, named her redheaded newborn Ginger. I started going by Gin as soon as possible, because it's really not great having people *ooh* and *aah* over your matching name and hair.

"Hey, Lauren," a male voice calls.

We both turn and see Sam Stockwell grinning at us. He's a football player with more swagger than substance.

"You two gonna go munch some carpet?" He makes a V with two fingers and sticks his tongue between them. "Can I watch?"

"Fuck you," Lauren says in a bored tone. "Go play with your balls."

"You wish you could play with my balls, lesbo."

He sneers, and Lauren rolls her eyes. I slip the straps of my backpack over my shoulders, and we start in the direction of the auditorium, where play practice will be.

"I'm parked in B lot," she says when we're almost to a set of side doors. "Text me later if you want."

"Okay, have a good night at work."

When I get to the auditorium, it's still empty. I'm usually the first one here, which is fine by me. I like to put in my earbuds and start painting scenery before I have to talk to anyone.

I could have spared a few minutes to hang out with Lauren, but I know she's going to smoke pot in her car before she leaves the parking lot, and I'm not into that. I sat in the car with her once when she did it and got a contact high and an ass-chewing from my mom when I got home that night. She said she could smell the pot on me from ten feet away.

The fall play is a modern retelling of Cinderella. Instead of a raggedy dress and bonnet, the heroine wears uncool clothes from a department store. She overcomes the scorn of her classmates and wins the heart of the prom king in her sparkly gown, which makes him finally see what he's been missing in her.

Lame, I know, but I was outvoted on every objection I voiced. It pisses me off that a guy is always considered the ultimate win for a girl. I wanted Cinderella—or Ellie, as we call her in our version—to skip the prom, attend a great school on a full scholarship, and make the *Forbes* list by age thirty.

Instead, I'm painting an abstract fireplace hearth, which Ellie gives her monologues in front of. I'm digging all the shades of black and gray I get to work with.

"What the shit, Gin?" a dark voice booms so loud I can hear it over my music. "Did you spill black paint all over your head again?"

I pretend I can't hear Jack Pearson, the biggest, loudest asshole on the football team. He's got a comment for everything, and people are afraid not to laugh at his jokes because they don't want to become the butt of them.

It's not like I haven't heard people talking about my hair all day anyway. Last night, I colored it the darkest color they carry at the local drugstore—a shade called Midnight. It's darker than the black I usually color my hair. My mom even raised her brows when she saw me, and *nothing* fazes her.

"Hey, what's up?" another male voice says.

My spine tingles with awareness at the sound, even though the question isn't directed at me. Chase must have come by with Jack before football practice today. I casually turn down the sound on my phone so I can hear the conversation. My back is to them, but I'm pretty sure Chase is talking to Madison, who has the starring role in the play. Even in her costume of Kmart jeans and a frumpy top from the Salvation Army, she's still gorgeous.

"I took notes if you need them," Chase says to her.

She responds, and he laughs, the deep tone of it making me warm all over.

"I have to pay attention in that class," he says. "Calc kicks my ass."

I feel the dig of an elbow against my arm. "Hey, what am I supposed to do when I get here after practice?" Jack asks me.

Glaring at him, I pull the earbuds out of my ears. "I'll still be here, so I'll let you know then."

"Oh, that's right." He grins. "You have no life."

For some stupid reason, our football coach makes his players volunteer to help with extracurricular activities that aren't as popular as football. And in Roper, that's all of them. Working on scenery used to be my escape, but it's only the second week of the school year, and I can already tell that won't be the case this year. I'm stuck babysitting Jack, who just spends his time here running his mouth.

"What is *this*?" a shrill voice cries.

I'm all too happy to put down my paintbrush and walk away from Jack to see what Amanda is upset about. Like me, she doesn't say much, so if she's bothered about something, that's unusual.

"Well, *someone* did it," she's saying sharply as I approach.

The two freshmen boys who work under her are both giving her frantic shoulder shrugs and head shakes.

"What's going on?" I ask.

"Someone cut a hole in one of the lockers." She points at her set, a row of lockers she's been meticulously detailing since the first day of school.

Sure enough, there's a golf-ball-sized hole in one of them, stage lights shining through it as they're being tested behind us.

"You like it?" Jack asks from behind me.

The amused swagger in his tone grates on my nerves hard. I try not to engage with stupid, but right now, I can't help myself.

"You did this?" I demand.

"Hells yeah." He grins. "It's a glory hole."

"A . . . glory hole?" I'm taken aback by the bounds of his stupidity threshold.

"I wish I had one in my locker," he says with a self-satisfied nod. "I'd just stay in there all day getting my rod sucked by girls walking by."

"You're such a fucking idiot!" Amanda's tearful tone makes me turn back to her. "I've spent so many hours on that, and you just ruined it."

"Whatever, fatty." Jack rolls his eyes at her. "I wouldn't want you to suck my dick, 'cause you'd probably put some ketchup on it and try to take a bite."

Chase scowls in Jack's direction as Amanda's face morphs from pink to deep crimson. I turn to Jack, point my finger at his chest and prepare to unleash my fury, but I'm interrupted by Mr. Douglas, our school's history teacher and theater advisor.

"Jack, get to practice," he says sternly. "And clean up the language because next time, I'm telling your coach."

Jack nods, his expression sober now. I give him a sullen glare as he turns to walk over to Chase and Madison.

"Gin, I need to pull some people off to work on posters," Mr. Douglas says.

"I thought the cheerleaders were doing them."

He smiles wryly. "Apparently, there were some issues with last week's football game posters, so we've been asked to do them from now on."

I roll my eyes. "They're just giant rolls of paper you paint words on. How hard can it be?"

"I've been given a directive." He shrugs. "They need to be neat, colorful, and say more than just 'Roper Rocks.'"

"Perfect," I deadpan. "So they send us football players who not only aren't helpful, but damage our scenery, and we have to send our best painters to make rah-rah posters?"

"Do you want to head up the poster-making?" There's amusement in his tone.

Mr. Douglas isn't from Roper, and he understands my disdain for the obsession with all things football here.

"Pass," I say, putting my earbuds back in and walking back to my set.

Chase is still talking to Madison, his blue eyes dancing with amusement. When he follows Jack out of the auditorium, I can't help staring after his broad back, hoping he'll glance over his shoulder and see me.

But after more than a decade of attending school together, that's unlikely.

He's the quarterback of the football team, but Chase isn't like Jack. He doesn't make fun of people. He looks out for his two younger sisters and gets good grades. Chase will have a football scholarship to the school of his choice when he graduates.

But Jack will end up living here his entire life, because guys like him can't handle the realization that they aren't a big deal outside of their hometown. He'll be wearing his letterman jacket into his thirties, reliving the glory days at the local coffee shop.

And me? I'll be far away from here in New York City. My mom can visit me there if she wants to keep living in Roper. In nine months, I'm leaving for good, because I don't belong here, and I never will.

two

Chase

IT'S GAME DAY. BEFORE I'VE even turned off the alarm on my phone, I know from the smell of cooking bacon. The churn in my stomach isn't from hunger but from knowing I'll lead my team onto the field in twelve hours.

I'm not nervous—that's never been my thing. But I'm also not complacent. Winning requires the constant awareness that nothing is a given. Being the quarterback of a team that hasn't lost a game in more than a decade comes with its own set of mental challenges.

When I walk into the hallway and see that the bathroom door is closed, I knock on it to let my sister Cassie know I need in. It's always her hogging it, never Alyssa. Cassie's a sophomore, and she's got the hots for one of my teammates, who knows better than even to look in her direction.

"What?" Cassie demands.

"You know what. Hurry up." My voice is deep and gravelly

from sleep.

"I have to finish my hair. I need ten minutes."

I shake my head in frustration. "I only need five. Can I get in there real quick?"

"Go eat breakfast, and I'll be done after that."

"I have to shower first, Cass." I glare at the closed door. "I'll just wait. Hurry up."

Sharing a bathroom as a family of five wasn't much of an issue before my sisters were teenagers. Monday through Thursday, Dad leaves for work at the steel mill before sunrise, so he's in and out before we're even up. Mom's not much for primping. She gets in and out, like Alyssa and me.

Leaning my back against the wall, I run through highlights from film of our opponent tonight. I've watched more film than usual this week because the Jefferson City quarterback switches up his plays often. With some guys, I know what to anticipate. But I remember the Jefferson City quarterback from last year. They scored on us. I have to be ready for him.

I get lost in thoughts of the game, and it seems as though hardly any time passes before Cassie opens the bathroom door and walks out, her fruity, powdery scent making me cringe. It lingers in the bathroom too, so I make quick work of showering, still running through film in my head and remembering Coach's comments as we watched it.

Football isn't just about beating the opponent for me. When you play for Roper, you have to be aware that your greatest opponent is yourself. I want to lead my teammates to a win that is smarter than our last one. The more decisive, the better.

When I walk out of the bathroom, Alyssa is standing in the hallway waiting for her turn, her acne face wash in hand. She's at the awkward thirteen-year-old stage, and no matter how many times I tell her it'll get better, she doesn't seem to believe me. She just rolls her eyes and tells me I wouldn't know the first thing about being awkward.

Not on the outside, maybe, but I do know what it's like to feel different. I'm lucky I can keep that to myself, though, unlike Alyssa.

I head downstairs, and as soon as I walk into the kitchen, Mom gives me a big smile.

"Hope you're hungry," she says.

"Always."

I take in the spread on the table—bacon, eggs, oatmeal, and whole wheat toast with peanut butter. Breakfast is always my biggest meal on game days.

Before I've had a chance to sit down, Mom is loading up my plate with three heaping spoonfuls of scrambled eggs, several pieces of bacon, and two pieces of toast. I reach out to take it from her.

"That's great, Mom, thanks."

"I'll get you a bowl of oatmeal too."

"Just a small one."

She smiles as she heads for the stove. "I'll cut up a banana and put it in your oatmeal."

"I can do that."

She lowers her brows as she spoons oatmeal into a bowl. "Just let me do it, Chase. This is the last year I get to."

The sadness in her tone hits me right in the gut. For the past thirteen years, life in our house has revolved around me playing football. It's not just during summer training and the fall season, either. In my off-season, I play seven-on-seven. Once I started high school, my dad started taking me to recruiting camps.

Next year, I'll be playing college football. And though we've never talked about it, I know my family won't be coming to watch those games. Any school I end up accepting a scholarship to will be far away from Roper, Missouri, and they won't be able to afford the travel.

My parents don't have to tell me they're behind on bills—I can tell. Mom's car has been sitting idle in our driveway with the transmission out for almost three months now. She drives Dad to work every morning and picks him up every afternoon. Cassie and Alyssa had to buy their own school clothes this year with babysitting money.

The one thing they've never cut back on is my football. It's expensive to play at this level—trying to land a spot at the best colleges to get drafted from—especially for a family with just one blue-collar income. The camps, travel, and equipment cost a mint. I can't contribute by working much, because my focus is on football year-round.

It'll all pay off when I make it. Not in the way my dad thinks, though. He doesn't take me to camps and watch my practices because he's proud of me. He didn't coach my teams when I was playing Pee Wee football because he wanted us to do something fun together.

My dad wants to see me succeed where he failed. At least, that's how he sees it. Eighteen and a half years ago, this was his life. He'd led the Roper football team to a state championship and had his choice of scholarships to the best colleges when he got his girlfriend—my mother—pregnant.

From the moment I was born a boy, he's seen me as his chance for redemption. He's in for a hell of a surprise, though. I'll make it, all right. And before the ink on my first pro contract is dry, I plan to get my mom and sisters away from him. He's a mean asshole. It's another one of the things we all know but never say out loud.

"This is really good, Mom."

She's standing silently over the stove, her head bowed. After a few seconds, I realize something is wrong.

"Mom?"

"I'm fine, honey." She waves a hand at me, but I can hear the tears in her voice.

I set my fork down, my mood darkening with anger. "Did something happen?"

She shakes her head vigorously. "No, I'm fine, Chase."

But still, she won't look at me.

"Did Dad say something to you? Or do something? Did he hurt you again?"

She turns and looks at me, her eyes wide with alarm.

"No," she says in a hushed tone. "No, it's nothing like that."

"I've never seen you cry for any other reason." My jaw tenses as I remember an incident last week.

She sighs heavily. "Let's not talk about that, Chase."

"What's wrong, then?"

Tears well in her eyes again as she meets my gaze across the table, her standing on one side and me sitting on the other.

"I'm just proud of you. And not because of football. You'll be turning eighteen in two months, and I know you'll be a good man. You have a good head on your shoulders and a good heart."

"I got those things from you."

Her smile fades. "Your father wasn't always like he is now. You remind me so much of him sometimes."

"I look like him, but I'm not like him."

"You have his confidence."

I shake my head, my appetite gone now. "I have my own confidence, Mom. I'll never be like him."

"He's not all bad."

My tone is low and serious as I say, "Don't make excuses for him."

She's about to say something else, probably in his defense, when I hear Sam pulling his truck into our driveway.

"Gotta go," I say, picking up my backpack from the floor. "See you tonight."

"We'll be there." She tucks her blond hair behind her ear. "Have fun out there tonight."

I smile and nod, though we both know this season isn't about having fun for me. I had fun freshman year. My sophomore year, everything changed when I became the starting quarterback. That role goes with me everywhere. I'm the face of our team, and I try to be a deserving one.

"Hey," Sam says when I open the passenger door of his truck and get in.

"Hey."

"Ready to kick some Jefferson City ass tonight?"

"You know it."

He turns up the country music he loves on the drive to school. I hate it, but it's his truck, so I never say anything. Sam and I have been friends for so long that we don't have to talk just to fill the silence anyway. I run through my playbook in my head, remembering what Coach told me to watch for in the Jefferson City defense tonight.

It's only a five-minute drive to school, and when we park and walk through the main doors, a couple of freshmen players are there waiting for us, both wearing their red Roper jerseys since it's game day.

"Hi," one of them says to me, his voice cracking.

He licks his lips nervously and passes me a long bundle of tissue paper. I arch my brows with amusement as I take it.

"How much paper did you wrap it in?" I ask him.

"Two packages . . . sir."

I pat him on the shoulder. "What's your name?"

"Jimmy, sir."

Poor kid looks like he's about to puke. His friend is shuffling his feet nervously, apparently afraid even to look at me.

"Jimmy," I say, "you don't need to call me sir. I know the sophomores like to scare you guys, but don't fall for their bullshit. It's just Chase, okay?"

He nods. "Yes, s—Chase."

I unroll the layers of tissue and take out the single red rose that was being so carefully shielded.

"Good job, Jimmy." I hand him the wadded-up tissue paper.

"Who is it?" His words come out in a rush, his voice breaking again.

Damn. I did not sound that bad when my voice changed.

"You'll have to find out with everyone else," I tell him.

Several other varsity players join Sam and me, and we all head for the wing where the upper-class lockers are located. Everyone will be hanging around there, waiting to see who's getting this rose.

It was a unanimous vote by the team last night. This is only the second game of our season, but because we played some scrimmage games before the season started, it's our fourth rose.

This may be my favorite part of being team captain. All eyes are on me as I walk down the hall. Every girl I make eye contact with gives me a hopeful grin. And the grins fade when I walk past them.

"The cheerleaders stepped up their game on the posters," Sam mumbles next to me.

He's right. The posters hanging in the hallways this morning are the best I've ever seen. They're colorful and neatly lettered.

When I slow my walk, then stop and turn to a group of three juniors pretending to talk casually in front of some lockers, everyone goes quiet. This Friday morning football season ritual will be the talk of the school today.

Who's getting this rose? That's what everyone is dying to know.

"Taryn," I say to a hazel-eyed brunette.

Her eyes brighten, and she swallows hard.

"Chase." She clutches the books in her arms so hard the color drains from her knuckles.

"This is for you." I hand her the rose, and she breaks out into a huge smile as she takes it.

"Thank you."

"See you tonight?"

"Absolutely."

I wink at her and lead the team back down the hallway, hearing her friends squeal happily as soon as our backs are facing them.

Sam elbows me and gives me a wicked grin. "Solid choice, man."

"What, did you forget who we picked or something?"

"Nah, I just forgot what a great body she's got. Volleyball players have the best asses."

I shove his shoulder. "First things first, brother. We've got a game to win tonight."

He laughs. "It's your job to worry about that."

He's right. And it's not just winning I have to be concerned about, but my own performance too. I have to bring my A game tonight, because there'll be at least one scout in the stands.

There are only thirteen games left in my high school career. And I have to make every one of them count.

three

Gin

THE ONLY SCHOOL LUNCH I refuse to eat is the pizza. It's an affront to pizza to call the cardboard squares with glistening grease on top by the same name.

And since I forgot to pack a lunch on this pizza Friday, I'm starving by the end of the school day. I jog out to my Toyota Camry, toss my backpack on the passenger seat, and hit the nearby McDonald's for a cheeseburger and a strawberry shake.

I eat the sandwich on the drive back to school, and when I park in a vacant spot near the main entrance and grab my backpack, there's a crowd gathered on the sidewalk.

Ugh. Probably a pissing match over whose pickup truck has a louder engine or something.

I keep my head down as I pass the back of the group, because I just want to get inside to play practice. I've almost reached the wide stone steps at the front entrance when the sound of a low female voice makes me stop.

"You better be crying, little girl. I'm gonna teach you to never look at him again, you hear me?"

It's the distinctive, deep voice of Rhonda Jameson, whom everyone calls Ronnie. She's a swimmer with broad shoulders and back muscles you can see rippling through her shirt when she walks. Like me, Ronnie is a senior. She's mean and vindictive. I imagine some poor freshman is peeing herself right now.

The crowd cheers as a girl cries out in pain. What a bunch of assholes. They've got their camera phones out to record someone's hurt and humiliation. That's the Roper way.

I keep to myself not because I'm intimidated by my classmates, but because I have nothing in common with most of them. I'm not afraid to intervene—I can't stand by and do nothing as someone's about to get their ass kicked by Ronnie.

Pushing my way through the crowd, I'm disgusted as I hear Ronnie laughing at her victim's tears.

"Not so bad now, are you?" Ronnie leers at her.

I get to the front of the crowd and see it's Cassie Matthews that Ronnie is apparently planning to beat up. There's a bright red handprint on Cassie's cheek, and she's cringing as Ronnie pulls her hair back.

Ronnie spits in her face, and the crowd responds with sounds of shock and glee. Cassie's expression is pure terror.

"Enough," I say, handing my half-empty milkshake to the person next to me and stepping forward.

"Nowhere near enough," Ronnie says with a sneer. "Get the hell out of here, Gin."

"Leave her alone. You've made your point."

My face heats with a mix of disgust and anger. It's the curse of being a redhead—I blush at the drop of a hat.

Ronnie lets go of Cassie's hair, and Cassie exhales deeply.

"She can't be your girlfriend," Ronnie says, turning her attention to me. "She was trying to get with Ryder at lunch today. Or does she swing both ways?"

I'm not responding to her insinuation that I'm gay. All I want to do is get out of here and get to play practice.

"Take it up with your boyfriend, not her," I tell Ronnie.

Ronnie arches her brows, amused. "I'll take it up with whoever I want. She's got this coming, so you better fuck off while you still can."

She turns back to Cassie, who cowers in fear. Ronnie is stronger than a lot of the guys at Roper. She broke a guy's arm last year when he accidentally touched her ass in the hallway.

"Leave her alone." I move to stand between Cassie and Ronnie.

"All right, now you've pissed me off, Gin."

Ronnie tries to brush me out of her way, but I dig my heels into the ground and crouch down. I'm only five foot six and a hundred and ten pounds. Ronnie's got at least fifty pounds on me, but I'm not letting her get past me.

"Get out of here, Cassie," I say over my shoulder.

Ronnie's lips part with shock. Rapid footsteps pound the pavement behind me, and then Ronnie's look morphs into an angry scowl.

"You dumb bitch," Ronnie mutters.

She grabs two handfuls of my shirt and throws me to the ground. The impact knocks the breath out of me. I haven't even been able to refill my lungs with air before Ronnie is on top of me.

I put my arms over my face as she punches. She's heavy, her weight pressing down on my rib cage, and every blow hurts like a mother. The crowd is loving it, cheering and encouraging her.

She pulls one of my arms away and lands a hit to my nose. I cry out in pain and reach wildly toward her, hoping to poke her in the eye or something.

My hand just finds empty air. I've been in exactly zero fights in my life until this moment. And right now, I'm more worried about Ronnie's weight on me than her hitting me. I can't breathe.

"No more, Ronnie," a male voice says from behind us.

The weight is pulled off of me, and I suck in a deep breath. My English teacher, Mr. Winters, is holding a snarling Ronnie by the back of her shirt.

"Gin?" He looks down at me, confused.

"Yeah."

I put a hand on my nose, which is burning with pain, and warm blood coats my skin.

Mr. Winters shakes his head in disgust. "I have to get her inside. I'll be right back for you, Gin. Don't move."

He takes Ronnie away, and the crowd starts to thin. Not one person offers me help.

I'm planning just to lie here and wait for Mr. Winters, but then I hear footsteps pounding on the pavement. A second later, Chase is leaning over me.

"Gin? *Shit.*"

His dark blond hair is glistening with sweat. He looks even better close up than I've imagined. There's a faint outline of gold stubble on his face, and his eyes are the bluest blue I've ever seen.

He gets down on a knee and puts his arms beneath me.

Holy. Shit. Chase Matthews is touching me. I'd enjoy it more if I weren't in so much pain.

With one arm beneath my back and the other beneath my knees, he scoops me from the ground effortlessly. Cassie comes over then, her cheeks streaked with tears.

"I got my brother because I didn't know what else to do," she says breathlessly. "I'm sorry, Gin . . . and . . . thanks for what you did."

I should respond—really, I should, but all I'm able to do at the moment is stare at Chase's profile. He's got that focused look in his eyes as he carries me around to the side of the school.

"Go home, Cass," he calls over his shoulder. "I'll take care of her."

He bends down to open a door, inserting a foot in the opening and using it to open the door wide enough to walk through.

"You're bleeding on the floor," he says, lowering his brows in thought. "Can you reach my waist? There's a sweat rag there. It's clean; I haven't used it yet."

He smells like the sweet spice of deodorant and aftershave. I take in a deep breath of his scent as I awkwardly reach down for his waist. And I touch his upper thigh, followed by . . .

"Oh God!" I pull my hand back, eyes wide with horror. "I'm so sorry."

A corner of his mouth crooks up in a grin. "Relax, Gin. That was just a football pad."

I want to die. Right here and now. I just took out a billboard for my inexperience by mistaking a football pad for a penis.

"Here," he says, crouching down in a squat. "See if that helps you reach it."

I lean up a little and see the white washcloth-looking rag, a corner of it tucked into his waistband. I grab it and press it to my nose.

Chase stands back up and continues walking. I could tell him that he doesn't need to carry me. I probably *should*, but . . . I don't. This is the stuff my girlish fantasies are made of.

I don't seem like the sort who has girlish fantasies, and I would never admit to them out loud. But deep inside the most secret corner of my heart, I've been hiding a major crush on Chase

Matthews for years. There was something about him that stole my heart in childhood, and I've never gotten over it.

He opens the locker room door the same way he did the other one, and I'm immediately hit by the smells of soap and sanitizer.

"There's no one in here," he says. "The whole team's on the field warming up."

He carries me into another room, away from the lockers, and lays me down on some sort of padded table.

"Keep putting pressure on it," he says, walking over to a cabinet.

He takes out supplies—a couple more white cloths, gauze, and a bottle of liquid. When he walks into the main locker room area, I take advantage of the opportunity to look at him. I could occupy quite a lot of time just looking at him in his formfitting white pants. His legs look strong, and his ass looks . . . well, grabbable. It's defined and tight, the pants giving me a better look than I ever imagined I'd have.

He returns to the room I'm in, and I notice that on top, he's wearing a red T-shirt that says "Roper Football" in white letters. One shoulder is stained darker red with my blood. I'm a total creep for liking that for some reason.

Standing next to the table, he reaches for the cloth on my nose and says, "Okay, let's have a look."

After setting the bloody rag aside, he dabs at my face and nose with a clean, wet one.

"Ah." I flinch as he touches my tender nose.

"Sorry," he says softly. "I'm trying to go easy."

"It's okay."

When I was a kid, I had a crayon in my box called "Denim." That's the color Chase's eyes are close up. I study them as he focuses on wiping the blood from my face. His eyes are framed with thick, light brown lashes, the color a little darker than his hair. He has a tiny freckle next to his left eye.

"Are you hurt anywhere else?" he asks, his eyes focusing on mine now.

"Uh . . . no." I don't think so anyway. I can't admit to him that since the second he arrived, I haven't been able to think about anything but him.

He picks up one of my arms, running his fingertips up and down my skin as he examines it. A crackle of electricity runs from the tip of my spine to the base and then back up again. I've never been touched by a guy, and being touched so tenderly by Chase has my heart pounding wildly.

"You sure?" He sets down my arm and then picks up the other one, examining it. "How'd you end up on the ground?"

"She . . . um, threw me."

His brows lower with concern. "You want me to look at your back? It's fine if you'd rather I didn't, but if you're hurt there, I can go get our trainer and have him check it out."

"Uh . . ." My face flames hot as I think about pulling the back of my shirt up for him.

"It's okay," he says, laughing softly. "But you should have your mom look at it later."

He picks up several pieces of gauze and hands them to me, saying, "In case your nose starts bleeding again."

I clutch the gauze in one hand as he takes my free one and slides his other hand behind my back, helping me sit up on the table.

"You feel light-headed at all?" he asks, his brows pinched together with concern.

I shake my head.

"Gin." My eyes meet his, my stomach fluttering over the way

his deep voice sounds saying my name. "Thanks for stepping in like you did to help my sister."

"It was no problem." I shrug and smile awkwardly.

"She said no one else helped her."

"You know how people are."

He presses his lips together and nods. "Yeah. But you helped her. Ronnie could have pounded the shit out of you, you know."

I smile weakly. "Yeah, I'm hoping my first fight was also my last."

"Do you need help getting home?"

I slide down from the table, remembering where I'm supposed to be right now. "No, I need to get to play practice."

He runs a hand through his hair, puts his hands on his hips, and gives me a skeptical look. "You need to go lie down and get some ice on your nose. It's starting to swell."

Well, that has to be really attractive. I look down at the ground, suddenly self-conscious.

"I'll be okay."

"Gin, seriously." Chase tears open a small paper package. "I want you to take this Tylenol and go home to ice your nose."

"I guess it would be bad to get blood on the scenery I'm painting."

He nods and walks to a small refrigerator, taking out a Gatorade, opening it, and handing it to me.

As he drops the two Tylenol tablets into my hand, his fingertips brush across my skin, sending a warm pulse of excitement that hits every nerve ending in my body.

I take the medicine, and he grins his approval.

"I'll walk you out to your car. Tell me if you start to feel light-headed, okay? You lost a decent amount of blood."

He walks beside me, opening doors so I can walk through

first and looking down at me every now and then to see if I'm okay. I'm relieved we don't talk, because what would I say? I'm way out of my comfort zone here.

I'm not one of those girls who wants to make a play for Chase. He doesn't see me that way, and I know it. I'd be mortified if he ever knew about my crush on him. The silence between us allows me to remain the cool and collected Gin everyone knows me as. Yes, there is a miniature gymnast doing a floor routine in my stomach right now, but he doesn't need to know that.

Chase even opens my driver's side car door for me.

"You sure you're okay to drive?" he asks as I slide into the car and dig my keys out of my backpack.

"I'm fine. Thanks for your help."

He looks down at me for a couple seconds, seeming to need to decide for himself if I'm okay.

"Okay," he finally says. "Text me when you get home so I know you made it." He pulls out a cell phone and says, "What's your number?"

My mouth goes dry, and I swallow hard. I have to remind myself that this isn't him wanting my number for real. It's him wanting to make sure the girl who just got punched standing up for his sister gets home okay.

I give him my number, and he types out a message.

"You've got my number now. Text me when you get home."

"I will."

He closes the door, and I start my car. My heart is pounding as I pull out of my parking spot, forcing myself not to look at Chase again.

That was surreal. I can't believe any of it happened. It was the most words Chase has ever spoken to me, unless our group project on the gallbladder in seventh-grade science class counts.

I'm about to pull out of the parking lot when I grab my backpack and pull my phone out of a pocket. I can't help myself.

I look at the screen of my iPhone and see his message: *Hey, it's Chase.*

I'm fluttery again. Careful not to touch it so he doesn't get a read confirmation while I'm still in the parking lot, I set my phone down and focus on driving.

This is going to make for an interesting dinner conversation with my mom tonight.

four

Chase

IT'S NOT UNTIL THE FINAL second ticks away from the clock on the scoreboard that I can finally breathe easy again. The Roper crowd erupts into celebration mode, and our team does the same.

"You were perfect out there tonight," Coach says to me, nodding his appreciation.

I don't know about perfect, but I was definitely in the zone. I had my mind on the big picture but didn't miss anything small. On game days, I've got lots of things running through my head—plays, Coach's words from practice the past week, my Dad's advice, my knowledge of what the other team does best . . . but the opening game kickoff brings me complete clarity. I'm focused then, never nervous.

And once a game is over, I'm mentally exhausted. I could go for a long, hot shower and a nap, but there's no way I can blow off the after-game party for that.

"Hell yeah!" my teammate Tony Granger yells as he wraps me in a tight embrace.

He lifts me up, letting out a primal victory cry. I smile and let one out myself. We have a lot to be proud of tonight. No one more so than Tony. We shut out Jefferson City, due mostly to Tony's performance on the defensive line.

"You killed it tonight, man," I say in his ear.

He's about to respond when a cooler full of ice and water is dumped over our heads by a couple teammates. I shake my head, and droplets of water fly through the air. The cold water feels good.

When we get to the locker room, I'm not surprised when Coach names Tony the game MVP. I get a little emotional as we all cheer for him, because Tony's coming into his own this season. He's a senior who used to be a kick-ass follower but has stepped up to be a leader his senior year.

Our trainer makes me sit in an ice bath because I took a hard hit during the game. I get out when he's not looking and head for the shower. I'm drained, and I want to make my appearance at the party and then get home to bed.

The team's after-game parties are epic. We have them at the lake house owned by Skylar Adair's parents. Skylar's dad owns several car dealerships in town and is loaded. He pays a cleanup crew to come in every Saturday morning and restore the lake house to its pre-party condition.

The lake house is on the outside of town, away from neighbors, so we can be as loud as we want. There's an unspoken agreement with the local police that they'll leave us alone as long as no one gets hurt and no one drinks and drives.

I've been coming to these parties since I joined the varsity team as a sophomore. It's the only chance the team gets to blow off steam away from the field, and we make the most of it.

I ride to the party with Sam, and as soon as we walk in, someone hands us each a red Solo cup full of beer from a keg. Sam downs half of it immediately. I take a sip of mine, already planning to dump it off somewhere.

To stay in peak condition, I can't drink alcohol. But I try not to be obnoxious about it because the other guys like to get stupid drunk after games, and I don't want them to think I look down on that.

Hell, I wish I could have that mind-set. But for me, there's no room for error.

"Hey, did Taylor say if she was coming?" Sam asks me, raising his voice to be heard over the noise.

I shrug. "I don't know."

"See if she texted you."

I give him a look. "Why would she text me?"

"She's got a thing for you."

"No, she doesn't."

He rolls his eyes. "Will you just fucking check, Chase?"

I take out my phone and look at the screen. Just a video message from the cheerleaders congratulating me from the girls' locker room and a text from an unknown number. Lowering my brows, I read the message from the unknown number.

I made it home fine. Thanks again for your help.

It comes back to me then. The message is from Gin, and I saw it before the game started but didn't open it. I'm glad she's okay. I owe her for helping Cassie like she did.

"Who was that?" Sam grabs for my phone, eyes widening as he clicks on the video message. "Whoa."

Several of the cheerleaders are wearing nothing but bras and their skirts in the message of congratulations. Sam seems to have forgotten all about Taylor as he watches it.

A loud cheer erupts from the other room, and people head that direction. Sam and I follow. When we walk into a bedroom, I see Tony's already enjoying the biggest perk of being MVP this week. He's standing at the foot of the bed, holding on to Taryn's ankles and groaning as he fucks her.

She's loving it. This is why every girl wanted that rose this morning—it means being the team's virgin sacrifice this week. Roper girls save their virginity, hoping to be one of the sixteen girls we pick each season.

As MVP of both preseason games, I got to be first with Alexis Bushnell and Mandy Smith. I like that Tony's getting his turn now.

"You think she'll let me in her ass?" Sam asks me.

I give him a skeptical look. "Can't hurt to ask, I guess."

The crowd gets louder as Tony hits Taryn harder and faster. Looks like he's ready to finish already.

"Ladies first!" a deep voice yells out.

Tony grins and reaches down to touch Taryn. I tell the guys it's unclassy to get off with no concern for your partner, but sometimes they need reminding.

"You going next?" Sam asks me.

I shake my head. "Go ahead."

The yells and chants are getting louder, and I leave the room to get a bottle of water from the kitchen. Seeing the newest member of the Sweet Sixteen give it up used to be exciting for me, but I'm kinda over it. I was part of it thirty-two times between the past two years. It's fun for the newer guys—and for the girls.

I only have twelve games left in my high school career now. Twelve more roses to give out on Friday mornings in my second year as team captain. I'm sure I'll take advantage of the opportunity for no-strings sex again, but tonight, I'm too sore and tired.

Oftentimes, other girls watching the players take turns with the newest member of the Sweet Sixteen want their own turns with us after. It turns into a literal clusterfuck some weeks, and I don't have the energy tonight.

I'm thinking about hanging out in the hammock down by the water when I see Ryder St. Clair in the other room. I'm suddenly not so tired anymore.

Gripping my water bottle in my fist, I walk into the living room. Ryder has an arm around Ronnie, who's giving him a smug smile.

"Hey," I say to Ryder.

"What?"

"You better keep your girl away from my sister."

He laughs. "I can't control this one, man. She's got a mind of her own."

"If she comes near my sisters—or Gin—ever again, I'm not gonna kick her ass for it," I tell Ryder.

"Yeah, you better not."

"I'll kick *yours*."

He sneers, and I clench my right hand into a fist.

"Look, I think it was all a misunderstanding," Ryder says. He turns to Ronnie. "Right, babe?"

She glares at me. "Tell your sister to stay away from my man."

"It's pretty loud in here," I say to Ryder. "Why don't we go talk about this outside?"

He puts his hands in the air, his expression serious now. "No need for that, man. I hear you."

"Do *you* hear me?" I ask Ronnie.

"Yeah, whatever."

There's a loud, collective cheer from the bedroom. Tony must have finished. My mind's not on that, though. I'm still scowling at Ryder and Ronnie.

"This is the only warning," I tell them.

"You can't get into fights," Ronnie says, sliding an arm around Ryder's waist. "What would happen if our golden boy football god got suspended?"

I arch my brows and shrug. "If Ryder gets his ass beat, it won't be by me. He'll get in his car one night, and someone will pull a hood over his head and take him out in the country, where he'll get the shit kicked out of him by someone he never even sees."

"That won't be necessary," Ryder says, his eyes wide with fear. "Ronnie's not gonna give you any more trouble."

"Good."

I walk away then. I'm so pissed off over what that brute Ronnie did that I'd like to punch her boyfriend just for the hell of it, but I need to choose my battles.

I'm not in the mood for a party. I text Sam that I'm walking home. It's only a couple miles. I need time to myself to think about things.

There were people watching that fight today who I thought were my friends. I saw the videos posted on social media before the game started. People who should have stood up for Cassie just laughed, getting more excited as things escalated.

But Gin Fielding, who hardly knows my sister or me, took a punch to the face for her. Cassie was shaking when she came to get me from the field this afternoon. I hate to think what Ronnie could have done to Cassie—or Gin.

I owe Gin more than some Tylenol and a thank-you. But she's so quiet and disinterested in everything around her. All I know about her is that she paints scenery for school plays and swims at the local Y. She only has two friends and mostly keeps to herself. What would a girl like her even want?

five

Gin

I SET MY LUNCH TRAY down on the table, and Lauren immediately reaches for a fry. I pass her the paper boat full of fries and the chicken sandwich I got for her, and she dives in.

When I told my mom during freshman year that Lauren never had lunch, she started giving me double lunch money. I always buy two of everything and just set the food in front of Lauren. We don't need to talk about it or anything.

Raj is right behind me, setting his lunch tray and backpack on the table.

"How's it going?" he asks us.

"Okay," I say.

"Your nose feeling better?"

I nod. "It's been three days. It's not really even sore anymore."

He looks over at Lauren's notebook, where she's holding a pen over a blank page. "Whatcha workin' on?"

"It's a list of everything I don't hate," she deadpans. "I just finished it."

I snort-laugh and twist open my bottle of water.

Sam Stockwell is walking past our table with Clay Houser, another football player, and he looks over at us and says loudly, "So two dykes and a terrorist walk into a lunchroom . . ."

Clay howls with laughter. We ignore him. It has to be so much worse for Raj than it is for Lauren and me. I know no one actually believes we're lesbians; it's just their running joke. But a lot of people in Roper are leery of Raj—short for Raja—just because he's Middle Eastern.

He's not even a practicing Muslim. Raj's parents died in a car accident when he was a toddler, and in their will, they gave his father's former college roommate and best friend custody of their son.

They couldn't have chosen better. Dr. Jim Walker and his wife, Melanie, are great people who have two biological children. They love Raj as their son in every way, and their kids consider him their brother. He feels the same about them. At school, though, he's always been an outcast. It wasn't until junior high that he started hanging out with Lauren and me.

Lauren leans in and speaks in a low tone. "Did you guys see the Friday night gang-bang video?"

I wrinkle my nose at her mention of the back-door app the videos are posted on. "I never watch that garbage."

"I watch that garbage every week," Lauren says with a shrug. "It makes me feel good about me, seeing girls so desperate for validation that they let the football team gangbang them in public."

"Well, it makes me sad."

Lauren rolls her eyes. "Sad for bitches like Taryn and Carmen? Actually, they're all bitches. It's part of the football team's selection process. They want popular, bitchy virgins who think they're the shit."

"It's gross." I take a sip of my water and shake my head. "And no girl deserves to be treated that way."

"They're there because they want to be," Lauren says with a shrug.

"So, Raj, how's calculus coming?" I ask, eager to change the subject.

He sighs heavily. "It's hard. I have a ninety-two."

"A ninety-two?" Lauren scoffs. "You're kicking ass."

"I'm dangerously close to a B."

"You crack me up. Like a B would be the worst thing that could ever happen."

"It is when you've got a 4.0," Raj mutters.

"You two are gonna be famous someday." Lauren looks back and forth between us. "A superstar artist and a rocket scientist doctor. I'll be able to say I knew you way back when."

"I'll never be famous," I say wryly. "And that's fine by me."

"Don't sell yourself short, Lauren," Raj says. "You've got just as much potential as we do."

She laughs and rolls her eyes. "Yeah, right. I'll end up in this dumpy little town for the rest of my life, sacking groceries or something."

"You can do anything you want to do," I tell her for at least the hundredth time.

We don't discuss it much, but Lauren doesn't have an easy life. It's just her, her mom, and her younger sister. I think she feels an obligation to stay in Roper and help take care of them since money is tight, but she's never come out and said it.

Raj works on a calc paper while Lauren and I eat and talk about the movie marathon we're planning for this weekend. Despite her tough-girl exterior, she's just as much of a sucker for a love story as I am, and we're going to binge watch *The Notebook*, *The Princess Bride*, and the show *Felicity*.

I'm laughing at something Lauren said when I hear a voice behind me that makes my skin prickle with awareness.

It's Chase. I don't turn around, but I unconsciously sit up straighter and tuck my hair behind my ear. Not that he's going to look at me or anything.

But for once . . . he actually *does*. He's passing by my table with a couple of football players, and he turns my way. Our eyes meet, and I feel mine widening with surprise. The corners of his lips crook up in a smile, and he holds my gaze for a full two seconds before turning to get into the lunch line.

Just that one glance has my heart pounding wildly and my cheeks flushing with awareness. Lauren knows about my crush on Chase, but Raj doesn't, so she just smiles at me and says nothing.

Nothing's different between Chase and me. He appreciated me helping Cassie, that's all. I was invisible to him before and now he's aware of my existence, but it doesn't mean he likes me or anything. I tell myself that until my heart slows to its normal pace.

But still, there's a small shred of hope in my heart. Maybe he's seeing me in a new light. And if not—even if he never does anything but look at me—I'll happily soak up those looks.

My desperation is a little disgusting, I know. I'm annoyed that of all people to have a secret thing for, I chose Chase. He's the golden boy quarterback. I'm sure he stars in the fantasies of most of the girls in this school.

And if there's one thing I'm not, it's a conformist. I wish I could have a crush on some obscure guy no one else notices. Like Raj. He's a great guy, and he doesn't gangbang girls just because he can. At least, not that I know of.

The thought makes me laugh. Raj is definitely a virgin. Some girl will be lucky to end up with him someday, but he just doesn't give me that fluttery feeling I get from being near Chase.

At least my feelings are safely locked away in my heart. Lauren would never tell a soul.

When Chase walks by again with a lunch tray in his hands, I force myself to appear preoccupied with my phone. My flaming cheeks will give away my feelings if I'm not careful.

I'm mindlessly scrolling when I get a message from Lauren.

He looked at you again.

And like that, my heart rate flies right back into overdrive.

RONNIE GOT SUSPENDED FROM SCHOOL over our fight, and people are still staring and whispering when they pass me in the halls. The freshmen who work on the theater crew are in awe of me, which is funny. At least, until they ask me to tell them what happened for the third time. Then I put in my earbuds and ignore them.

We finish practice early because Mr. Douglas has dinner plans. It's the first time I've been home before five since school started.

The driveway that leads to our house is made of stone, and Michael, the local guy Mom hires to do maintenance on our house, is on his hands and knees scrubbing the stones with a brush as I pull in and park.

"Hey, Gin. How's senior year treating you?" He looks up at me as I step out of my car.

"It's good. How are you?"

"Can't complain." He grins and goes back to work.

Michael is in his fifties, and he's been taking care of our house for almost ten years. It's his full-time job, because our house is . . . well, enormous. It's a ninety-year-old red brick mansion that was built by an oil tycoon back in the day. All the woodwork is original, and Michael painstakingly cleans and polishes every bit of it.

The oil tycoon was named Richard Olney, and the Olney Mansion is the reason we live in Roper. Mom found out it was for sale, and the beauty and history of the sprawling six-bedroom house spoke to her. Twenty years ago, she bought it. And around eighteen years ago, she went to a sperm bank and picked out my father.

I don't actually know him, but she tells me he was handsome and had a great smile. She doesn't know him either, because the sperm bank protected his identity. He was a research scientist with auburn hair, blue eyes, and no genetic predisposition to any serious diseases.

So, obviously, I look like him, which is weird since we'll never meet. But I made my peace with it a long time ago. It's been Mom and me forever, and I can't imagine it any other way.

"You're home early," Mom calls out from the kitchen when she hears me walk in.

"Practice let out early," I call back as I set my bag down.

I walk through the sunroom, filled with potted plants that Michael waters and carefully dusts, and then the large living room, complete with an antique piano Mom bought with the house even though no one ever plays it.

When I walk into the kitchen, Mom is peering over the dark rim of her reading glasses, looking at a cookbook propped up on the counter.

"What are you making?"

"Hmm?" She looks up at me. "Oh, chicken and dumplings."

"Yum."

"How was school?"

"The usual."

She brushes some flour from her hands and reaches for her wooden rolling pin. There are flecks of flour in her dark curly hair, and I brush them away as she rolls out dough.

"If you needed to hide a body and a deep freezer wasn't an option, what would be your next choice?" she asks me, her brow furrowed as she concentrates on her task.

"Depends. How long will it be there?"

She considers. "You aren't sure. But you need to hide it well."

"I guess . . . bury it?"

"No, because the dirt would be disturbed, and someone would see it."

"Hmm . . . trunk of my car."

She shakes her head. "That's too clichéd."

"It's clichéd for a reason. It's a good hiding place."

Morbid conversations like this are a regular occurrence in our house. Mom's real name is Julia Fielding, but she writes thriller novels under the name JD Morris. JD Morris is one of the top five grossing authors in the world. I'm proud of her, though I wish she'd work less and give a social life a chance. I worry about her being all alone when I leave for college. She doesn't need to write anymore, we're set for life, but it's such a part of who she is that she does it for love of the stories.

"How's the book coming?" I ask her.

"Still plodding along." She sighs. "I just can't figure out what to do with this body."

I take a bag of tortilla chips from the pantry and open it. "Famous last words, Mom."

She smiles. "How's the fireplace coming along?"

"It's almost done. I'm pretty happy with it. The glowing embers are the best part."

"So what will you paint next?"

I suppress an eye roll. "An abstract pumpkin."

"Oh. How will you make a pumpkin abstract?"

"That's a great question. One I've asked Mr. Douglas a few times. He just waves his hands around and talks about swirling colors."

"If anyone can pull it off, you can, Gin."

I shake my head as I reach for another tortilla chip. "We'll see. Surprisingly, this whole reboot of Cinderella is actually really good. The script, I mean."

"Madison Grayson is Cinderella, right?"

"Yeah. And when she remembers her lines, she's good."

"Well, I can't wait to see it." Her eyes sparkle with happiness as she looks at me. "I'm just so proud of you."

"I just paint scenery, Mom. It's no big deal."

She gives me a pointed look over the rim of her glasses. "Artistic talent is a very big deal."

"Hopefully, NYU will think so."

"I'm positive they will."

I roll up the top of the bag of chips and put it back in the pantry. "I'm sending in my application next month. Remember you promised me you wouldn't use your influence to get me in."

Her sigh is flustered. "If that's what you want. But considering the amount I've donated to that school—"

"Mom, you promised."

"I know." She puts her hands in the air, feigning innocence, and bits of floury dough drop down onto the kitchen counter.

I love her belief in me, and so many other things. She stops writing every day to cook a nice dinner, no matter how intensely she's into her manuscript.

Wrapping my arms around her from behind, I give her a hug.

"Do you need help?"

"No, thanks. But will you run out and ask Michael if he'd like to stay for dinner?"

"Of course he will. He loves your cooking."

"Just ask him anyway."

I was right—Michael wants to stay for dinner. If nothing else, I guess Mom will have his company when I leave for college. But I already know it won't just be her who misses our nightly dinners together. I will too.

MY BLOOD IS PUMPING EXTRA hard this morning. It's not just tonight's game I'm excited about, but also the rose the freshman player just handed over to me.

I don't usually look at the roses, but I did this time. It's a long-stemmed rose, its perfectly shaped bud of petals a deep shade of red. I even took a sniff of the sweet, perfumy scent.

This rose is special. It's going to change everything for Gin.

For the past week, I've paid attention to her. Where she goes, what she does, who she's with. She rarely talks to anyone besides Lauren and Raj. She doesn't even look at other people, and others don't look at her. It's like she's invisible, her head down as she just bides her time.

It makes me appreciate what she did for Cassie that much more. For an introvert to step in like that . . . I know it had to be harder for her than for someone like me.

I'm guessing she'll blush like crazy and not be able to find any words to say when I hand her this rose. Everyone will be shocked, including her. It took me a good forty minutes to convince the rest of the team we should pick her.

One thing I've realized from paying attention to Gin this past week is that she's actually pretty. She's got pale blue eyes and a bright smile. I imagine her body's nice under those baggy clothes, too. The inky black hair isn't helping her out any.

Doesn't matter, though. I'm not doing this because of her looks. I want to repay her for what she did for my sister, and this will change her entire senior year. Being one of the Sweet Sixteen will elevate her social status like nothing else could. She'll be the envy of most every girl at Roper, and the guys will see her in a whole new light.

Sam falls into step beside me as I make my way down the hall to Gin's locker, the rest of the team following behind me.

"You sure about this, man?" he asks under his breath.

"Yep."

He lets out a sharp breath. "Yeah, but she's—"

"Don't. The vote's done, and there's no going back."

He glances over at me. "But if we could go back, would you want to?"

"No."

With my tone, I let him know the conversation is over. Sam's never cared who was chosen for the Sweet Sixteen before. One of his favorite things to say is, "Pussy's pussy." I don't know what's got his panties in a bunch over Gin.

The farther I walk down the hall, the more people stare, all of them holding their breath. The hallway smells like powdery perfume, some of the girls spraying it and putting on lipstick as I approach.

They're all hoping it's their day. My gaze passes over them

like they aren't even there, landing on the back of the girl bent down to pull books from the bottom of her locker and put them in her backpack.

Gin's oblivious to the rose ritual, and that makes me almost smile. She's gonna be blown away.

The rest of the team hangs back as I stop and approach her. I keep the rose half hidden behind my leg as I stand in front of the locker next to hers.

She doesn't look up, her attention focused on the pages of a notebook she's flipping through. There are at least a hundred students in this hallway, and they all just fell into silence. Gin doesn't even seem to know.

"Gin?"

She looks up at me, pulling earbuds from her ears. "Did you say something to me?"

"Yeah." I run a hand through my hair and grin. "Can you, uh . . . stand up?"

She stuffs the notebook into her green canvas backpack and stands, looking off to the side and then back at me, her eyes narrowing as she figures out everyone is watching us.

"What's going on, Chase?"

"I have something for you."

A slight pink flush colors her cheeks as she furrows her brow at me. I take the rose out and hold it in front of her. There's a collective gasp from the students around us. Pretty overdramatic, because obviously, I was planning to give the rose to her.

Gin's eyes go wide, and her cheeks darken to red. "What . . . the hell . . . ?"

"It's not a joke," I reassure her, because she's looking anything but pleased.

I should have known she'd think it was some kind of prank.

Gin's been teased and called a lesbian since middle school.

"Um . . . it *is* a joke, though." Her eyes meet mine, her chin tipped slightly up.

"No, it's not. I chose you, Gin. You're one of the Sweet Sixteen."

She scoffs and shakes her head. "I most definitely am not, Chase. Choose someone else."

When she turns back to face her locker, I can feel the energy in the hallway. It's trapped, everyone frozen in disbelief.

"Gin," I say in a low tone. "I give you my word this is legit. Take the rose."

She shakes her head again, silent.

I keep my shit together. This isn't unfolding like I imagined it would, but I can fix it. I reassess and try a different approach.

"You're a beautiful girl. Why wouldn't we choose you? I want everyone else to see you the way I do."

Her eyes are narrowed when she turns to face me, but I can still see they're a darker shade of blue than usual.

"I'm sure everyone would see me differently if I allowed myself to get gangbanged by the football team, but I'm fine with the way I'm seen now, Chase."

Her tone is level and firm, and the hallway fills with the buzz of whispers. Sam is muttering his disgust nearby. This thing is going to hell fast.

"It's not gangbanging, Gin." My aggravation bleeds through in my tone.

"Really?" Her brows shoot up in mock surprise. "Maybe you should Google *gangbanging* sometime."

There's a shocked laugh behind me, and a muscle in my jaw flexes unconsciously.

"Take the goddamn rose, Gin," I say through gritted teeth.

"No." She holds my gaze in challenge.

Now I'm pissed. I'm doing her a favor, and this is how she thanks me? I shove the rose toward her.

"Just take it, and we can talk about this later."

"I don't want your stupid rose." Her voice rises with anger. "No self-respecting girl would. Go find some desperate wannabe groupie."

The mood in the hallway has shifted. The shocked whispering has turned into an angry rumble that may explode at any moment. Gin and I are staring each other down, me willing her to accept the rose and her telling me to fuck off with her eyes.

Gin shoulders her bag and moves to step around me. I can't let my big idea blow up in my face like this, so I step to the side too, blocking her path.

"Will you please take the rose, Gin? Please. I'm asking you to do this."

Her eyes are glistening with tears, but she's not sad. I realize as she stares up at me, chin tilted defiantly, she's furious.

"Take that rose and shove it up your ass, Chase."

She walks around me, ignoring the glares and insults that await as soon as she's a few feet away from me.

I push off the locker with my shoulder, pissed off as I stride through the crowd of teammates gathered in the hallway. The cluster parts into two for me, and I stalk off in the direction of my own locker.

"What the hell was that?" Sam falls in beside me, his tone alarmed.

"I don't want to talk about it."

"You want me to give the rose to someone else?"

The warning bell rings. We have two minutes to get to class, and I only have a few seconds to make a decision.

Cut our losses, give the rose to another girl, and pretend the Gin incident didn't happen? Or keep trying to convince her to take the rose so I can salvage a shred of my wounded pride?

"No," I tell Sam. "I'll take care of it."

"Take care of . . . how? Do we need to vote again?"

I silence him with a look. "I've got it."

He nods and slows his pace. Everyone scatters, heading to class, and I stand in front of my locker for a minute, collecting myself.

That was a disaster. She turned me down. Gin Fielding told me to shove the rose up my ass in earshot of dozens of people. I'll never live this down.

And worse, a Roper tradition hangs in the balance. If I don't fix this, and fast, there's a lot more at stake than my ego.

Seven

Gin

I'M STILL SHAKING. EVEN AFTER skipping my first class to shut myself in a stall of the girls' bathroom and get myself together, my emotions are running just as high as they were an hour ago.

Maybe higher, actually, because I've been thinking things through. I'm still mad as hell that Chase thought I'd want to be one of the football team's vapid virgin sacrifices. His participation in the weekly gang bang is the one thing I've had to overlook to sustain my crush on him. The whole thing is sexist, offensive, and disgusting.

Then there's the way I was caught completely off guard by the whole thing. I was just standing at my locker, thinking about what books I needed for the morning, when suddenly half the school was staring at me as Chase tried to get me to take that rose.

Completely mortifying. And after the way I defended his sister, that's not what I expected from Chase. He'd assured me it wasn't a joke, but how could it not be? I'm nowhere near the social circle of girls who hope to lose their virginity to a bunch of drunken football players. I don't want to be either, but at Roper, no one would believe that. Everyone at this school thinks all guys aspire to be football stars and all girls aspire to date them. Or get gangbanged by them. It's all the same in this hayseed town.

At the sound of excited female voices entering the bathroom, I realize I completely missed the bell.

"I heard she paid him five hundred bucks to pick her," one voice says.

"No way."

"Yeah. She wanted it to look like he's into her."

Laughter fills the room. I close my eyes, my face flushed even though I'm safely hidden in a stall. Though I know the entire school is probably talking about me right now, I really don't want to hear the conversations.

"You guys?" I recognize the high-pitched sound of Devin Morton's voice. "Why would she do that? Gin's a lesbian. I know that for a fact."

I roll my eyes. Devin's a gymnast who considers herself the Roper gossip authority. She pauses for dramatic effect and then continues.

"She checked me out when I was showering after gym one day. It was so gross. She was staring at my snatch and practically drooling."

The cackles and groans of disgust make me sigh heavily. Devin's a liar. I don't go anywhere near the showers after gym class. I keep my head down, change clothes on the other side of the room and hope deodorant will be enough to get me through my last class without smelling. No public showers for me—gross.

"Chase is pissed, though." I'm not sure who the voice belongs to, but I can't help listening to it over the noise of others starting to fill the bathroom. "He just stared straight ahead during first period and didn't talk to anyone."

"He's got a right to be pissed," Devin says. "I can't imagine any girl saying no to him, but *Gin Fielding*? Seriously?"

I clench my fists, resisting the urge to throw open the stall door and tell Devin to go fuck herself. The last thing I need is more attention. What I really want to do is walk back out the front doors of the school, drive home, and never come back.

I can't, though. I'm too practical to even consider it. Even skipping first period was a big deal for me. As the voices start to filter out of the bathroom, I leave my stall of safety, shoulder my bag, and take a deep breath.

As soon as I walk out of the bathroom, the staring and whispering begins. I pass Raj on my way to class, and he gives me a quick nod and mouths, "You okay?" All I can muster is a half-hearted shrug.

I'm not okay. Chase Matthews just ruined my plan to lay low until graduation and then silently make my way out of here. Thanks to him, the entire school is talking about me. I'm done admiring him from afar. As of now, I despise him.

LAUREN NARROWS HER EYES AT me in disgust as soon as she sits down across from me at our lunch table.

"What the hell?"

I shrug as I pass items to her from my lunch tray. "I've asked myself that same question at least a hundred times today."

"It took balls to say no to him, Gin. Good for you."

"It's not like I could ever say yes," I scoff and shrug.

She arches a brow in consideration. "If it was just Chase . . . I'd probably do it."

Raj gives her a disapproving look as he sits down with his tray. He turns to me with a weak smile. "Hey. How's it . . . you know, uh . . . ?"

"I'm here." I meet his eyes and he nods.

"I'm sorry," he says.

"It's not your fault."

"But still, it's—"

He's interrupted by a sharp female voice. "Hey, Gin."

I look over my shoulder and see Melanie Pearson glaring at me, a couple of her friends snickering beside her. Melanie is a cheerleader and a devoted football-team groupie. I'm sure she's got something rude to say.

"What?" I glare at her impatiently.

"Are you really a lesbian, or are you just frigid?"

"I'm just not interested." I hold her challenging stare.

"Not . . . interested?" Her eyes widen, and she laughs humorlessly. "You mean because they have dicks?"

Lauren turns to her. "Did you know you don't *have* to let every guy in the school stick his dick in you? Novel concept, I know."

"I'm not saying every guy in the school." Melanie rolls her eyes, crosses her arms, and looks between Lauren and me. "But Chase? He did you a huge favor, Gin. Huge. And you just—"

"Tell him you'll take the rose," I say with a shrug. "I don't want it."

"You can at least be honest and admit it's because you're a lesbian."

I shake my head. "I'm not. I'd have no problem saying so if I were."

She gives me a confused look. "Well, it's not like you're super religious and saving it for marriage. What's the deal?"

Several people have stopped to eavesdrop. I sigh heavily and scowl at Melanie.

"Look, I just want to be left alone."

"Is your vag deformed?" a male voice in the small crowd calls out.

There are several cackles. I could swear I hear a growling noise from Lauren before she stands up and dismisses everyone with a sweeping gesture.

"Fuck off, trolls. Go find some desperate whore to take the rose or something." Her eyes narrow slightly, and she raises her voice. "I mean it, assholes. Fuck the fuck off."

Everyone leaves. Raj is eating in silence, trying to look invisible as he nibbles at his sandwich.

I know that feeling. Wanting to be invisible. I don't belong at the center of today's Roper High School gossip. All I do here is show up, do my thing, and leave. I deserve to be left alone.

But instead, people are still staring and whispering. I eat my lunch in record time, keeping my expression impassive as I get up, dump my garbage, and walk across the cafeteria to leave. I'm called a bitch and a prude, but I ignore it, shoulder my backpack, and put my earbuds in.

There aren't many places in the school I can go to be alone. After this morning, I'm over the Lysol-scented bathroom, so I head for the theater. I'll go backstage and paint for the last few minutes of lunch hour.

As soon as I start walking down the locker-lined hallway, I replay the rose thing in my head. My only regret is not telling Chase to go fuck himself as soon as he looked at me. What was he thinking anyway?

I'm a nice person, despite what my inky black hair and lack of a smile may imply. I don't talk about people, and I stand up for those who need it. I teach swim lessons to kids who need them for free. I'm a strong person but not a tough one. I couldn't hurt another person for anything. It seems really unfair that I'm the object of such disgust and scorn over this rose thing.

What's the big deal anyway? So I don't want to give it up to the entire football team. Why can't they just pick someone else and move on?

I'm almost at the end of the row of lockers when I feel a hand on my shoulder. I turn and see Chase, his expression stone-cold but his blue eyes dark with what looks like anger.

It's all I can do not to shove him. How does he have the balls to be *angry* with me?

"What?" I demand, pulling out my earbuds and glaring at him.

"Can we talk?"

There's a firm set to his jaw. I've only seen him wearing this expression, with a fire raging in his eyes, in football photos. This is the "fear me" look he gives opponents to intimidate them, I'm sure. It won't work on me.

"If you plan to lecture me, don't bother. You have absolutely no right to be upset with me, Chase, and I have every—"

"I'm not upset with you, Gin."

"What's with the look, then?"

"What look?"

I wave a hand, gesturing near his face. "The thing with your jaw, and your eyes . . . the look."

"There's no look."

I arch my brows. It's not like I can tell him I know all his expressions from years of crushing on him, but it's the truth. I probably know his moods better than he knows them himself.

"Okay." He gives a slight nod and looks away. "Maybe there's a look, but it's not directed at you. Not like you think it is anyway."

"What more could you have to say? I just . . . Why would you do that to me?"

I hate how thick my voice is with emotion and the burning in my eyes from tears I'm holding back. As angry as I am, I'm also hurt, but I don't want him knowing that.

"Gin—"

"You're an asshole." I clear my throat and steel myself.

He sighs heavily, meeting my gaze again. "Can we just talk?"

I shrug. "Talk. I'm right here."

Chase glances up and down the hallway, turning back to me when he sees it's empty other than the two of us. Still, he steps closer and speaks in a low tone.

"I was trying to do you a favor, and things just went to hell this morning."

"A favor?" I gape at him in disbelief. "How is that a favor?"

His look of aggravation says it should be obvious. "You know, to help you . . . get noticed more."

"Noticed?" I hiss. "Noticed for spreading my legs for the entire football team?"

"It's not like that."

"It is, though, Chase. It's exactly like that."

A vein in his neck stands out slightly as he scowls at me. "So you've been there? You've seen what happens at the parties?"

"Everyone knows."

"Everyone *thinks* they know."

I cross my arms and narrow my eyes at him. "Enlighten me, then. If it's not a gang bang of a virgin, what is it?"

He rolls his eyes. "You make it sound so crass. It's not like we're all standing around switching off. And it's *consensual*. Everyone's enjoying it."

"Well, I certainly wouldn't be."

His eyes soften. "Because you're nervous? I can make sure it's me if you want, Gin. Only me."

My stomach flutters against my will. I've dreamed of Chase looking at me this way—*seeing* me, and only me, even if only for a moment. But not like this. Not because I'm offering myself up as his post-game celebration.

"No." I shake my head for emphasis. "I just . . . can't possibly."

"Is it . . ." Chase clears his throat, glances at the other row of lockers and then looks back at me. " . . . I mean, do you really . . . you know, not prefer guys?"

A fire ignites inside me. "I definitely prefer guys, Chase," I say hotly. "Just not drunken assholes who have no respect for others."

"No respect?" He shakes his head and gives me a disgusted look. "Gin, you don't have a clue. And you won't even give me a chance to prove it to you."

"A *chance*?" I clench my fists at my side. "You think I'd let you be my first, so you can show me that your sex game has some sort of meaning? It means *nothing*, except that football players are shallow assholes who can get their rocks off with any willing girl, and that girls don't have enough respect for themselves to want more."

"It's consensual, Gin, how do you not see that? There's nothing wrong with girls enjoying casual sex. Mia Kearney changed her mind in the middle last year, and I stopped, okay? I *stopped*. I'd never take advantage."

For someone who breezes through the hardest classes at Roper High, he's not all that smart. There are voices approaching as I say, "Look, it's not happening. Pick someone else."

"I can't—" He stops, wraps a hand around the back of his neck, and then looks at me again. "I don't want to. I want you to say yes."

"So you don't look bad in front of the whole school?" I ask bitterly.

He leans in. "So we don't *both* look bad, Gin. I didn't mean for any of this to happen. It was supposed to be a good thing."

"I'd much rather be called a bitch and a lesbian than go to that party." I hike my bag up over my shoulder. "Don't worry about me. Pick someone else."

The voices get closer, and Chase leans in so close that I can smell his woodsy scent. "I'm not doing that. I'm gonna play hard tonight, and I promise you I'll be the MVP. I promise it'll be me, Gin. Only me if you want. And I hope you'll be there after the game."

I scoff and shake my head. "I promise you I won't. No matter how good-looking you are and how long I've . . . never mind. It doesn't matter. There's no way."

People are looking at us now, slowing down so they can listen to our conversation. I slide my earbuds back in, turn my back to Chase, and leave.

Why do I feel a twinge of disappointment? I'm disgusted with myself. It's not that Chase wants me, but that he wants to save his reputation as Asshole Team Captain. I was right to say no. If he asked me a hundred times, I'd say no a hundred times.

Still, though. I never thought Chase Matthews would look at me that way. With intensity and desire in his eyes. I kind of liked it. I kind of liked it a lot.

eight

Chase

IT'S SO QUIET IN THE locker room that I can hear ice clinking into a tub a trainer is filling up. There's not as much pre-game swagger in here this week. We all know Lennox is a brand-new team this year. They have a new coaching staff and a new quarterback. From the scouting our coaches have done and the film we've watched, I know this isn't the Lennox I played the past three years. They're stronger and hungrier to prove themselves.

I'm sitting on a bench, elbows on my knees, getting my head into the right place. Between things with Gin and this game, I have no clue what happened in any of my classes today.

After parties and the Sweet Sixteen are far from anyone's mind in this room. We all have one objective right now—to win this game.

"Matthews." The booming call of my coach makes me lift my head and look across the locker room. "Out in the hallway."

I sigh heavily as I stand. I don't need this right now. There's only one person Coach would let me leave this locker room for. And as soon as I step out the door and it swings closed behind me, he starts in.

"McConnell is fast," my dad says. "Faster than you. He's also smart. So you have to—"

"I know." I stop him midsentence. "We scouted him."

Dad narrows his eyes at me. They're blue, like mine, but perennially a little bloodshot. He doesn't drink on Fridays during the season until after the games, but every other day, he starts in on the cheap canned beer as soon as he walks in the door after work. He's also just getting older. His stomach's not flat anymore, and his hairline's thinning out.

"Don't tell me you *know*." His tone is laced with disgust. "If you were so goddamn confident, you wouldn't look like you're pissing your pants right now. So shut up and listen. Get your pre-snap reads right. You screw those up, you're in deep shit."

I nod, because the last thing I need right now is to piss him off. If I do, it won't be me he takes it out on.

"Lennox is good at disguising their defense," he continues. "Stay sharp. Don't get lazy out there."

"I won't."

"There are scouts here tonight, Chase."

My chest tightens with pressure as he speaks. My focus will stay entirely on this game, scouts or not, because I'm part of a team. I'm not here to bring attention to myself. But now I'll know in the back of my mind that if I make even the slightest misstep, my dad won't let me forget it.

"I've got it," I tell him coolly. "I haven't lost a game yet."

He leans in. "Don't get cocky, boy. I've been watching the Lennox film."

I'm about to tell him I have too, but I just nod instead. He claps me on the shoulder, straightens his red Roper Football hat, and leaves without another word.

The farther he goes in the other direction, the more I relax. When I walk back into the locker room, no one looks at me. Everyone's in their own mental zone. Every player knows that in a game against Lennox, one mistake could lose the game. And in a town like Roper, no one wants to be the one to make such a mistake.

I learned over my years of playing football how to drown out the noise and excitement of the crowd when I need to. Sometimes I feed on it, other times I need to shut it out. Tonight is one of those nights it's just my teammates and me. We're a band of brothers on the field, all of us ready for battle but a little more sober about it than last week. I think we all just want this game to be over.

My pre-snap reads are all good, and we execute every play perfectly. But Lennox's defense is on point tonight, and they shut us down at almost every turn. These guys want this win—I can see it in the narrowed eyes of every one of them.

We're tied 7–7 at the half, and the stands are quieter than usual. Not every game we play is a blowout win, but we don't fall behind and we don't find ourselves tied with our opponent at halftime.

Until tonight.

I can feel the pressure crushing my shoulders as we all sit down in the locker room. When I exhale, it feels like the first time since before the game started.

"Matthews," Coach calls out.

I look up and meet his gaze, blinking away the sweat that rolls down my forehead and into one of my eyes.

"Is this about that girl? Are you thinking about whether you'll get laid tonight instead of this game?"

The air in the room stills. What happens at the lake house after football games isn't exactly a secret in Roper, but teachers, coaches, and parents don't *talk* to us about it, for fuck's sake. They look the other way and let us do our thing.

"No, sir." I sit up, palms on my thighs.

"Where the hell's your head, then? You're slow out there."

There's not much fire in his tone, because this isn't about me. I'm not slow, and he knows it. We've all done everything we're supposed to do. But our undefeated record is in danger, and someone has to get an ass-chewing for it. As team captain, I'm the clear choice.

"What about the rest of you asswipes?" he booms. "You worried about where you're gonna stick your dicks after this game? Because, boys, if we lose, there's not gonna be an after party."

None of us gives a shit about the after party right now, and he knows it. I'm not the only one on this team being scouted, and that's nerve-racking for any blue-collar son. We're the pride of our families, all of us, and that's what's really on the line tonight.

Coach slams his clipboard against some lockers, lectures us some more about getting our heads out of our asses, and then goes over plays again.

In the third quarter, we get a lucky break when one of Lennox's linebackers trips and falls, allowing Sam to score. After that, our mojo seems to come back, and we pull off a 21–7 win.

I'm relieved, but exhausted in every way. I think it's more mental than physical. Even though I played well, I feel responsible for our weak first half.

Though I'd rather be alone after the game, I can't go home. My dad will want to rip me a new one, and I'm not up for it. So I ride with Sam to the after party, my thoughts wandering to Gin as he talks about the game.

She made it clear—she's not coming. But I could see in her eyes that a part of her wanted to. I think she wants popularity more than she's willing to admit.

nine

Gin

I LIKE TO THINK I don't scare easily, but the sick feeling in my stomach as I linger inside my car in the high school parking lot Monday morning is definitely not from the toast I ate for breakfast.

When I took the weekend away from my phone and computer, I told myself it was because I wanted to unplug. Spend quality time with my mom watching movies and cooking. But truthfully, I didn't want to deal with texts and notifications about that stupid after-game party.

I'm hoping they chose another girl, had their ritual, and have all moved on from Friday morning. I don't care if anyone at Roper High School likes me—I never have—but I do want to be left alone. After all these years of flying under the radar, making myself nearly invisible, I didn't like the glares and whispers directed my way.

If I stay in my car much longer, I'll be late. With a heavy sigh,

I grab my bag, lock my car, and walk toward the front entrance. I keep my head bowed, my hair forming a dark curtain that conceals my face.

Someone mutters "Fuck her" as I walk up the stairs, but other than that, I manage to make it to my locker and then my first class without drawing attention.

When I walk into my second class, someone yells "Frigid dyke," and I feel my face turn hot with embarrassment. It's more of the same all morning. The one time I look up in the hallway, I see Chase walking in my direction on the other side, and I can't tell what he's thinking when our eyes lock. I flip him off so he knows what *I'm* thinking, though.

By the time I sit down at lunch, I'm starting to feel numb to the comments. Raj opens his mouth to say something, but I hold up a hand to stop him.

"You guys don't have to sit here." I look from Raj to Lauren.

"Why the fuck wouldn't we?" Lauren demands, narrowing her eyes.

I shrug. "I don't know. There may be collateral damage."

"Ha." Lauren takes the sandwich I pass her way. "I dare any cunt to approach this table and say shit to you. I'll cut a bitch."

"With what, a plastic knife?" Raj laughs.

"With my teeth if I have to. What the hell is wrong with this place?"

I take a bite of my sandwich, my shoulders sinking with relief at finally having my friends near. "So what did they end up doing at the party? Or should I say, who?"

Raj's expression turns serious. "You didn't hear?"

I shake my head. "I went radio silent all weekend."

"Can't say I blame you," he concedes. "They didn't pick someone else. Chase said they couldn't."

I roll my eyes and set my sandwich down. "It's like he wants to keep digging this hole deeper."

I'm covering my face with my hands when a male voice sounds next to me.

"Hey, Gin, you owe me a little something."

I raise my face and turn. It's a football player named John Hunt, and people are watching him with amused grins from nearby tables. He's rubbing his crotch and leering at me.

"You've already got a little something, John," Lauren says with a sneer. "It's called your dick."

"Lauren, I wouldn't even pity-fuck you," John responds. "You probably go for girls 'cause you can't get a guy hard."

"Go away, John," I say, my tone weary.

"Hey, Hunt, get your ass over here!" a deep voice booms.

It's Chase, and he's standing up at his table. All eyes turn to him. John seems to think about it for a second, but then he turns away and leaves.

I can feel Chase's gaze on me, and I warm against my will. I don't know what he's thinking. If he had good intentions when he tried to give me the rose, he should have smoothed things over by picking another girl and letting this die.

Instead, I'm still the subject of everyone's stares and snickers. Even a janitor gives me a long look as I'm pulling books from my locker at the end of the day.

When I get to play practice, Madison is running through a scene with Aiden, who is playing Prince Charming. I follow along, impressed when she gets almost every word right. Maybe she's been practicing.

I need to start working on the castle scenery. I'm inventorying my supplies backstage when a loud voice sounds nearby.

"There's the girl with the golden pussy!" Jack Pearson calls out.

He's coming my way, and my stomach churns nervously. Of all the assholes on the football team, Jack is the most volatile. He once physically assaulted a teacher who gave him a failing grade that benched him from a game. That teacher wasn't from Roper, obviously. Roper teachers know better. She "moved on to new opportunities" after that year, according to the school board.

"Think you're too good for us, Gin?" Jack stops right next to me, and there's no one else nearby but a freshman girl who scurries away as fast as she can.

"Leave me alone." I use a level tone and then turn back to checking my painting supplies.

"You like painting, huh?" Jack gets so close that I can feel the heat of his body next to mine. His proximity and his bitter, angry tone make my skin prickle with fear. "We won Friday night, so let's find a corner and I'll paint that red pussy white. How 'bout it?"

I feel close to vomiting, but I can't let him know he's getting to me.

"I'll pass," I say, shoving past him.

I walk over to Mr. Douglas, and I could swear by the look of pity he gives me that even *he* knows what's going on.

"I'm going to the paint store for supplies," I tell him.

He nods, and I grab my backpack and get the hell out of the auditorium as fast as I can.

I've almost made it to the safety of my car when a male voice sounds behind me.

"Hey, Gin."

I turn, fire racing through my veins as I meet the eyes of the tall, lanky guy walking toward me. He's walking slowly, because one of his feet is in a medical boot from an injury.

He's a junior, and I think his first name might be Ben, but I'm not sure. And of course, he's a football player. Seems every member of the team has a personal message to deliver to me today.

"What?" I demand. "I'm in a hurry."

His cheeks turn pink with embarrassment. "I just wanted to . . . I don't know . . . I guess, say . . . I'm sorry for what's going on."

The glare falls away from my face. I'm so shocked by his words that I don't know what to say.

"I don't, uh . . . think anyone should be treating you this way." He looks over his shoulder in both directions to see if anyone is in listening range. "I don't really think it's right, the whole Sweet Sixteen thing. Anyway . . . I just, uh . . . I'm only a peon so it's not like I can do anything about it. I just wanted to tell you not all of us are assholes. I know it doesn't mean much, but I'm sorry."

There's a lump in my throat. I can feel both his sorrow and sincerity, and it was the last thing I expected when I saw him walking toward me.

"That means a lot to me, actually." I clear my throat. "More than you know."

He nods. "It's because you're so strong, you know. That's why those guys hate you. You're the only one they've ever run across who's stronger than them."

"Hey, Hart!" A deep voice sounds across the parking lot. "Get your ass to practice!"

Once again, it's Chase. Ben's eyes widen, and he turns and hightails it toward the practice field, at least to the extent his boot will allow.

I open the door to my car and hear Chase calling my name. He's running toward me, wearing a worn, cutoff blue jersey and white football pants, helmet tucked under his arm.

I'm in no mood. I get in my car, lock the doors, and pull out of the parking lot without even looking his way.

~

FARNSWORTH HARDWARE IS A ROPER staple. Located downtown, it's the go-to place for everything from lawn supplies to car parts. It's housed in an old, crumbling building with shelves from floor to very tall ceiling.

"What can I help ya with?" a tall, burly man with a dark, silver-streaked mustache asks.

"I need paint." I pull out a list from my pocket. "And a few pieces of lumber if you have any scraps to sell."

"Right this way."

He pulls his green "Farnsworth Hardware" cap down as he leads me to the paint counter. I look through swatches and order the colors and amounts I need.

"You're part of that school play, aren't you?" he asks as he mixes. "Seen you in here a few times buying paint for it."

"Yes, I am."

"They send a boy to carry all this for ya?"

I shake my head. "Nah, I've got it."

"I'll help you get it all out to your car," he offers.

"That'd be great, thanks."

"I dated a girl in high school who was in a play once." He smiles at the memory. "Some Shakespeare thing."

"Oh yeah? We're doing a modern retelling of Cinderella."

He grunts his acknowledgment and moves on to the next gallon of paint.

Once he's mixed all my paint and rounded up some scrap lumber for me, he sets everything on the counter and puts on a pair of reading glasses, signing on to a computer.

"Let's see . . . this gets billed to the high school's account, right?"

"Right. I'm an authorized buyer for the Theater Department."

He scans through names on the screen. "What's your name, young lady?"

"Gin Fielding."

He immediately turns from the screen to look at me. "Gin Fielding? You're that author's girl?"

"Yes."

He narrows his eyes slightly. "Huh. I played football for Roper, you know. Class of '79. Best years of my life."

"That's . . . good."

The rolling feeling in my stomach sets in again. I look away, trying to focus on anything but his judgmental stare.

"Those are good boys on the team," he says gruffly, setting a paper on the counter with a pen. "They work damn hard to win for this town. Nothing wrong with them blowing off some steam."

I scrawl my signature on the paper and hand it to him. "I'll need a receipt, please."

Silently, he prints one off and hands it to me. Then he walks away, leaving me with five gallons and seven quarts of paint and a lot of scrap lumber.

It takes me seven trips, but I get everything loaded into my car on my own. And even though my sweat gives away my exertion, I don't let it show on my face. I even smile and wave at the asshole employee on my last trip out of the store.

This is exactly why I can't wait to get the hell out of here. But when I do, it'll be with my head held high. I may be hurting inside right now, but I'll never let the Roper faithful see it. They'd enjoy it too much.

ten

Chase

THE ROPER YMCA WEIGHT ROOM is almost empty. It's almost eight o'clock on a weeknight, which is my favorite time to come here. I don't like to lift weights in the high school weight room because I can't focus with the other guys screwing around.

"Hey, good game Friday," a bearded guy says as he passes me on his way out of the room.

I nod and get in position for bench presses. My shoulders are already worn out from drills at practice, but I feel like doing presses anyway.

Physical pain and soreness distract me from the thoughts racing through my head. When I got home from practice at dinnertime tonight, my mom had makeup caked on her face. She usually doesn't wear much makeup, and I instantly knew she was trying to cover up the black eye my dad had given her.

Wrong as it is, I was mad at her. Her fucking eye was so

swollen that no makeup could cover it up. How dumb does she think we are? She wouldn't even look at me, probably because she knew what she'd see on my face.

Rage. That's what I feel toward my father. All I want when I see her after one of his drunken episodes is to find him and tell him to give someone his own size a go for once.

He doesn't hit his kids. Only Mom. And afterward, *she's* the one who feels ashamed over it. He doesn't have the decency to feel remorseful.

Seeing her only added fuel to the fire inside me. I'm pissed off about all the crap Gin's been getting. I told the guys after practice that anyone who so much as looks at her wrong is getting an ass-beating from me, and I meant every word. The "favor" I did her has turned into a fucking disaster.

I knock out all my presses and move on to skull crushers. I've been here for more than an hour, but I'm in no hurry to leave. My dad was at the bar when I got home earlier, and I don't think he'll be home before ten.

He's been on my ass about committing to a school, but I put him off every time. I should've done it by now, and I know he's right that some schools will sign other players and I'll lose my shot at a scholarship with them, but I'm just not ready.

Part of me wants to get as far away from him as I can, but another part wants to stay close to my mom and sisters in case they need me. I don't know how to choose.

I wipe the sweat from my face, toss my towel into a hamper, and walk out of the weight room to hit the water fountain. There's a large indoor window that looks into the pool from the hallway, and I glance through it.

There's only one person in the pool, and she's wearing a modest, dark one-piece. She's doing the backstroke, water splashing onto her goggles and white swim cap.

She's graceful, her long, lean limbs not the build I'm used to seeing in swimmers. I stand off to the side and watch her as she switches to freestyle. I'm mesmerized by the smooth rhythm of her strokes in and out of the water.

I'm not sure how long I've been staring when I shake myself out of the spell I'm under. Just as I'm about to head for the water fountain, the swimmer climbs the pool stairs and slips off her goggles. I crane my neck, trying to get a look at her face, when she pulls off the swim cap and black hair falls around her shoulders.

Gin. My pulse races at the realization. The girl I can't seem to look away from is Gin.

She's not wearing dark, baggy clothes or a scowl. There's no black eyeliner. No clunky boots.

It's like I'm seeing her for the first time, and what I see is beautiful. She grabs a towel and dries her face, and as she walks toward the locker room, I get a good look at her.

Gin is gorgeous. I can't believe I've never seen her this way. Without that dark hair hanging in her face, I can see all of her for the first time, and it's making my breathing shallow.

A wave of shame washes over me. I blew it with Gin before I even knew I wanted a chance with her. I asked her to have sex with me and my teammates and got offended when she said no. She must think I'm a real asshole.

The realization hits me suddenly. I wish I could take it all back. I wish she didn't know who I really was. I wish she didn't hate me.

When she turns to look out the window to the hallway, my pulse races. Our eyes lock.

I'm expecting another middle finger salute, or at the very least, a dirty look. But she just holds my stare, water dripping from her hair and suit onto the tiled pool deck.

Something's happening to me. While standing on the worn-out carpet in the hallway of the Roper YMCA, I'm feeling something I've never felt before. It's intense. Heat floods me and longing consumes me.

I want to go in there right now. I want to run through the men's locker room and out to the pool, where I'll tell her I'm sorry. I'll tell her I get it. She's not just some girl. I'll get on my knees if I have to and ask her how I can make this right.

I can't, though. If I walk away from this window, she'll disappear into the women's locker room, and the moment will be gone.

She glances down at the floor, then towels off the dripping ends of her hair. I will her to look back up at me. I need to memorize her face like this—clean and fresh and completely uncovered.

I step so close to the window that my breath starts to fog up the glass. I stop breathing, just waiting for her to lift her chin.

Finally, she does. She holds my gaze as she wraps the towel around her waist. My tongue darts out to moisten my lips, my mouth dry.

What the hell is this feeling I'm having? There's no more drive to lift weights and bring on physical soreness to mask the stress inside me. If she'll just keep looking at me, just like this, everything will be good.

She moves to walk toward the locker room, and it's all I can do not to pound on the window and make her look at me again. I don't know what she's doing to me, but I know I don't want it to end.

When she gets to the locker room door and grips the silver handle, I take in her long, fair-skinned legs. Who knew she was hiding *those* under the cargo pants she wears?

She turns then, looking at me over her shoulder. I have to force myself to breathe.

I wish I could decipher what's going on in her eyes right now. What's she feeling? What's she thinking?

She slips into the locker room, and my heart sinks. The moment is over. I miss the feeling she gave me already.

I could wait for her in the parking lot, but I don't want to do or say anything that will ruin the moment we just shared. It was just a look, but it did something to me. *She* did something to me.

Does she know? Could she see it all over my face? Is that why she didn't look pissed at me for the first time since before the rose?

I don't even need to know the reason. No matter how unlikely it is, I have a flicker of hope that maybe she'll stop hating me. I'm not letting anything ruin it.

eleven

Gin

I DON'T THINK THE EARTH'S crust is all that interesting. A one-page paper about it would be okay, but three pages? Ugh. I push away my laptop and pick up my phone, unable to concentrate on my research paper any longer.

There's a text waiting on the screen.

Hey. I was surprised to see you swimming at the Y tonight.

I furrow my brow and read it again. It's from a number I haven't assigned contact information to in my phone, but I know who it is. It's Chase. I add him as a contact.

Why would Chase be sending me a text about nothing? At nine thirty at night?

I'm feeling testy, so I send a snarky reply.

Me: Didn't know frigid dykes can swim?

I stare at the screen, waiting for his response.

Chase: Gin . . . I hate what's happening to you because of me.

I soften as I read his words.

Me: It's not your fault. Roper's a small town with a small-town mind-set.

Chase: It is my fault. It's because of the rose.

Me: It'll pass eventually . . . right?

Chase: Yeah. If anybody gives you any shit, let me know.

Me: Ha—you'd be hearing from me every 5 minutes.

Chase: Are you serious?

Me: During school hours. But I'm over it, so it doesn't matter.

Chase: It does too.

Me: Why didn't you bang another girl? That woulda helped take the heat off me . . .

Chase: I was waiting for you to show up. Ended up waiting all night.

Me: Why? You didn't think I meant it when I said NO?

Chase: Hoped you'd change your mind.

Me: No fucking way.

Chase: Am I so bad? I would've made it good, ya know. Lots of kissing. Just the two of us.

My stomach somersaults, and I roll my eyes at myself. There's nothing romantic about that ritual, no matter how Chase's words make me feel in this moment.

Me: Yeah, followed by the rest of your team. No thanks.

Chase: What if it was just me?

Me: Still a no. You should celebrate winning with a pizza or something.

Chase: You make me smile, Gin. Want to go out for pizza with me?

Me: No. I gotta go, I have to finish my paper.

Chase: Another time, then.

Me: Or not. You aren't my favorite person, Chase.

Chase: Goodnight, Gin. See you tomorrow.

Me: Can't wait.

I put my phone back on the desk, screen side down so I'm

not tempted to look at it again. Is Chase just taunting me at this point? I think he's so not used to hearing no from a girl that he's taken me on as a personal challenge or something.

Ironic that my secret crush is now texting me for no reason. And it's just bizarre that he mentioned having pizza together. Chase seems to think he can charm me into changing my mind about this whole ritual gangbanging thing, but it's not happening.

Even though I know that's all this attention is about, I can't help liking it. I've dreamed of him noticing me for so long. His notice so far hadn't been what I had in mind—until tonight.

That look between us at the Y earlier is the reason I can't concentrate on the Earth's crust. Or anything else.

Since I was only wearing my black one-piece Speedo suit and I had no makeup on, I *should* have felt self-conscious. I *should* have gone running into the locker room for cover.

I couldn't, though. I was frozen in place, those blue eyes trapping me with their intensity. No one has ever looked at me the way Chase did tonight. I didn't just feel beautiful for the first time in my life in those few moments—I felt like the most beautiful girl in the world.

My heart had hammered more uncontrollably than it did the morning Chase offered me the rose. Even with the space between us and the barrier of the window, I'd felt something intimate passing between us. Something secret.

My cynical side wants to believe that look from Chase was just more of him trying to lay on the charm so I'll spread my legs for him and his teammates, but I know deep down, that wasn't it at all.

I can't even pretend to work on that paper anymore tonight. It's not due for another week, so I'll put it off. I look at the blinking cursor on my laptop screen, curious about whether the social media firestorm about me has died down at all.

Best not to even look. The few times I've peeked at social media since the morning of the rose, I've been so hurt and disgusted I had to turn away.

People can be such dicks. And this isn't even all that complicated. Girls at my school would say they're empowered. They've been taught about sexism and consent. So why don't they get that this after-game gang-bang party isn't an honor at all, but an objectification?

I consider texting Chase again to tell him I hate him and every other guy who takes part in that fuckery. He needs to know it was only a lapse in reason that made me look at him earlier without scowling or flipping him off.

It won't do me any good, though. He'll somehow read into it that I want attention from him.

Attention is the last thing I want from anyone at Roper High. I wish I would have followed through with my plan to graduate early and start at NYU a semester ahead of time. But the look on my mom's face when I pitched that plan made me reconsider.

I'm her only kid. She wants to see me walk across the stage and get my diploma on graduation day, and I don't want to deny her that.

I head downstairs to find something to eat. My plate of nutritionally void pizza rolls is slowly spinning inside the microwave when my mom walks into the kitchen.

"Hey, stranger," she says, grabbing a soda from the fridge.

"Hey, how's the book coming? Did you figure out what to do with the dead body?"

Her eyes light as she answers. "Thrown into an abandoned well."

I cringe. "Thank God it's abandoned, or that would be truly disturbing."

"How'd your abstract pumpkin turn out?"

"It's pretty decent." I shrug and return to staring at the microwave.

"Gin, is everything okay? You haven't seemed like yourself lately."

"I'm fine."

She pops open the can of soda, and after a few seconds, tries again. "I've never judged you when you come to me with things. I just want you to know—"

"Mom, I know." My voice has more of an edge than intended.

Several more moments of thick, tense silence pass. The microwave beeps and I open it, pulling out my plate.

"It's not *me* you'll judge," I say, sighing. "And . . . have you ever just wanted something to go away? This will just stir the pot further, and that's the last thing I need."

She slides onto a breakfast stool. "Stir it how? I'm not going to make you feel bad about anything, Gin."

The hurt in her voice stabs me. I know she'd never make me feel bad about anything. But she's been reminding me since I was a toddler that my body is my own, and anyone who tries to use or manipulate me deserves to be called out.

I can't stomach the idea of my mom stomping into my school with steam coming out of her ears, demanding to see the principal, football coach, superintendent, and anyone else in any position of authority. She'll be pissed that I was given a rose, yeah, but she'll be *livid* when she knows other girls take the roses and then get deflowered at a party in front of others.

"It's not you, honest." I bite the corner off a pizza roll to let steam escape. "It's everyone else."

"You've been withdrawn, honey. Angry. And I'm worried you need to talk things through. You have my word it stays between us."

I laugh humorlessly. "This one's gonna require a blood-signed contract."

"Are you pregnant?" she blurts.

"No."

Her shoulders sink as she exhales with relief. "Okay. My word is my promise. I've never broken that."

I pop the rest of the pizza roll into my mouth, considering as I chew. That's true—she's never broken her word to me. I trust my mom.

Leaning back against the counter with my plate in hand, I start talking. "You know Chase Matthews?"

"Of course."

Reluctantly, I tell her about how I intervened in Cassie's would-be ass-beating and how Chase patched me up after. The more I talk, the easier it gets, and soon the entire sordid story is pouring out of me.

Mom listens, her only reaction an occasional pursing of her lips. And after I finish by telling her about seeing Chase tonight at the Y and not hating him as much as I should, I pop another pizza roll into my mouth, waiting for her reaction as I chew.

"Well . . ." Her brows arch as she searches for words. "Wow."

"I know? Some fucked-up shit, right? Now you know why I ate all the mint chocolate chip ice cream."

A ghost of a smile touches her lips before she clears her throat and turns serious again. "I'm just devastated that this is happening. In my world, in my country . . . but in my little town? To my own daughter?"

"Nothing happened to me, Mom. My maidenhood is intact, promise."

Her lips part with surprise. "Not just that, Gin. That you were even asked to do something so *wrong*, it's just . . . *Chase* does this? The sweet blond-haired boy who loved the birthday cake I made you so much?"

"Mom, that was in second grade."

"I know, but . . ." She rubs her temples. "Okay . . . First, thanks for trusting me with this."

"You can't tell anyone," I remind her. "You promised."

She gives me a slow nod. "Yes, I did. And I'll keep my promise. I want you to know, honey, that there's a big world out there outside of Roper. You're being judged unfairly right now, but you did the right thing. I'm proud of you."

"I know. I'm not wondering if I should change my mind or anything, I'm just pissed at this point. People should leave me alone."

"But other girls . . . they say yes to this?" She grimaces with disgust and concern. "They *do* this Sweet Sixteen thing?"

"Yeah."

She shakes her head. "I can't . . . I don't even know how to reconcile that. I hate knowing it and not saying anything to them. Not letting them know they aren't expendable trash to be used for the amusement of a bunch of football players."

"Yeah, it's not the deepest bunch of thinkers who do this stuff."

"I don't care." There's conviction in her tone. "No girl should be treated that way, ever."

"I know, Mom. I do. But not all girls were raised by you. They don't know that."

"Well, can you—"

I put up a hand to stop her. "No. I'm not looking to save the world. I just want to survive my last year here, that's all. Girls at my school do stupid shit every day. You'd die if you knew what high school is really like these days."

She shakes her head. "I'm sure I would. And this is about you anyway. I'm sorry I got off track."

I set my plate of pizza rolls down on the island, pushing it toward her to offer her some. She takes one. Sliding onto the stool next to her, I take a deep breath.

"I just want to go back to being invisible. I keep my head down at school, you know? I don't ask for trouble. In Chase's fucked-up head, he was doing me a favor, and it ended up being the worst thing that's ever happened to me. I didn't think I could hate my school any more than I already did, but I was wrong."

"Oh, honey." Mom looks over at me. "I know you feel like you don't belong here, but I think you're wrong."

"Really?" I give her an incredulous look. "I have nothing in common with the people I go to school with. I don't like football, drinking cheap beer, or gangbanging, so that leaves . . . no one to hang out with."

"You have Lauren and Raj."

I nod. "Yeah, but even they aren't *like* me. Lauren doesn't think she can ever get out of Roper. And Raj . . . he's kind of afraid of his own shadow. I mean, I love them, but . . . am I making any sense?"

"Yes. I can't tell you how many times I've felt that way in my life. I feel like maybe I've passed it on to you, and I never wanted that."

"No, you just raised me to believe in equality, which is like a dirty word in this hick town."

Mom smiles. "You know why you belong here, Gin? It's *because* you're not like everyone else. You were the first girl who was brave enough to say no to that rose."

I smile back. "I think my exact words were 'you can shove that rose up your ass.'"

"That's my girl. And now other girls know that *they* can say no too. And those arrogant little pricks on the football team know not every girl wants to play their game. You weren't made to be invisible, Gin. Look at the way you stood up for Cassie Matthews when she was being picked on. You were made to change the world. And Roper is where you're starting."

I shake my head. "I haven't changed anything, Mom. Everyone hates me."

"It doesn't sound like Chase hates you."

I scoff. "I think he's just trying to charm me into changing my mind."

"Give it time. And no matter what, honey, don't let this change you. Don't let it make you bitter and angry."

"I keep hoping it'll die down."

"I'm always here if you need to vent. Or if you want to take a break from school, I'll go pick up your work and you can keep up from home."

I shake my head. "I'm not giving them the satisfaction of knowing how much it bothers me."

"I couldn't be prouder of you, Gin."

"Thanks, Mom."

"I do have to ask—do teachers and parents know about this? I don't understand how they can condone such a thing."

I shrug. "It's one of those things you don't know if they know about. It's not talked about with them. But that guy at the hardware store . . . he knew."

"Asshole."

"Yeah." I stand up and take my plate over to the sink, rinsing it and putting it in the dishwasher. "I'm going to bed. Thanks for listening."

"Always. I'll be up in my office if you can't sleep and need to talk some more."

"Okay." I walk over and hug her. "Night, Mom."

"Goodnight, honey. I promise this is going to get better."

I think about it on my way upstairs. Maybe she's right. When Chase gives another girl a rose this Friday morning, surely the focus will shift away from me. Not just the focus of the entire Roper student body, but Chase, too.

The thought gives me a pang of sadness, and I roll my eyes at how stupid I'm being. It makes me sad that Chase will be fucking some other girl this Friday night. What the hell?

She'll just be one of many to him. And that's all he wanted me to be, too.

Twelve

Chase

COACH CARTER COCKS HIS HEAD and gives me a confused look.

"You want to *what*, Chase?"

I shrug. "The other guys all do time, so I should too. And the drama department seems like a pretty painless place to volunteer."

"You're my captain, though. You have to put in more work than most of the other players. I don't expect you to sweat your balls off at practice, then dress people up in their . . . costumes or whatever those drama kids do, and then watch film and get your homework in."

"Just a couple of practices. I've got time. I don't want the other guys to think I'm getting special treatment."

"You sure you want drama? You don't want to make posters with the cheerleaders or something?"

I shake my head. "Drama's good. Tell 'em I'll be there tomorrow."

He gives me one more confused look before agreeing. "Okay, but if your game or grades are sliding, you're out."

"I understand."

I jog back over to run the next play at practice, doing it on autopilot. Jack Pearson paints scenery when he gets assigned to help the drama club, so hopefully that's what I'll be doing too. I'll paint anything if it means I can be near Gin.

After seeing her at the Y the other night, I can't get her off my mind. I've known her since kindergarten, but since offering Gin the rose, it feels like I've met a new girl. I'm intrigued and wondering why I've always written her off as quiet and disinterested in everything.

My mind is only half on practice, but that's enough. Coach is often telling me to dial it back at practice, anyway, and save my fire for game night.

I'm not feeling any fire this week. At least, not for football. When practice is over, I take a quick shower, eager to get home and finish my English paper. I'm pulling a clean T-shirt over my head when Jack Pearson's words make me freeze.

"That bitch needs her cunt thawed out. She owes me a fuck." He laughs, and some other guys join in.

I slam my locker door closed and walk over to him. "Who's that, Jack?"

His expression fades from a grin into a sneer. "You know who."

"Gin? 'Cause I distinctly remember telling everyone to leave her alone."

He shrugs. "Last time I checked, you weren't my daddy."

The room goes still with quiet. I step closer to him. "I'm your captain. And I'm not gonna tell you again. Leave Gin alone."

"What the fuck is up with you sticking up for her? She's a frigid—"

I shove one of his shoulders, and he stumbles back.

"Say one more word—" I point at him "—or go near her one more time, and you'll be sorry."

He scoffs and looks around at our teammates. Most of them are looking at the ground, the lockers—anywhere but at him.

"I see how it is." He laughs bitterly. "Bunch of fuckin' pussies."

I turn, grab my gym bag, and leave the locker room, not looking back. None of the other guys has said much about Gin—not to me anyway. Jack seems to have it out for her, though. He needs to let it go.

Usually, I catch a ride home from Sam, but today I don't feel like talking, so I walk.

Roper's small downtown is nearly full of locally owned businesses. Somehow, they hang in there, though most of the buildings could use some work. People here are loyal and willing to pay more to shop local.

I scan the windows of the sporting goods store, Peyton's. It's a sea of red inside, all jerseys and T-shirts supporting the team. Every pair of shoes I've ever owned has come from Peyton's. Same with my sisters.

I pass a dog groomer's shop, a hair salon, and a small diner that's full every morning. Occasionally, a business will close down, but someone always opens up another one in that spot. Nothing much changes in Roper, and I've always liked that.

Lately, though, I feel restless. I'm torn between wanting to get the hell out of here and away from my dad and needing to stay close to look after my mom and sisters.

I cross through the intersection leading from downtown to a residential neighborhood. All the houses are simple one- or two-stories with aluminum siding and maybe a one-stall garage. This neighborhood is a lot like mine, full of working-class homes most Roper kids grow up in.

There are a few exceptions—doctors and lawyers who build fancy houses on the outskirts of town, but for most of us, this is life. Not just life during childhood, but after that too. Kids like my dad make big plans to leave here after high school but then end up staying forever.

Not me, though. Whether I go to college near here or far away, I'm making it out of Roper. I'm going to give my mom and sisters a better life than they have here, and football is my golden ticket.

Kids from school wave at me as they drive by in cars their parents bought them. I've saved money from working in the football off-season, doing farm labor, construction, or any other odd jobs that require a broad back and strong arms. I've thought about buying a car, because it would make my life easier. But I'm afraid to part with the money. If my dad loses his shit some night and *really* hurts my mom, I know she doesn't have access to any money. He controls all that. My stash of cash would be enough to get my mom and sisters somewhere safe.

It takes me about half an hour to get home, and when I walk in, my mom is pouring something into a pan in the kitchen.

"Hey, whatcha makin'?" I ask.

"Cornbread, to go with chili for dinner."

"Sounds good."

She smiles. "How was p—"

"Chase." My dad walks into the kitchen, stops, and crosses his arms.

A bitter taste fills my mouth. I can hardly even stand to be in the same room with my old man anymore. But I can't let him see that, for my mom's sake.

"Yeah?"

"I got a call from the Bama coach today. They need a commitment."

The hairs on the back of my neck stand at attention as I try to figure out a response.

"I know we said either Ohio State or Bama," he says, "but I'm leaning toward Bama."

He said either Ohio State or Bama. I've been seriously considering FSU, because Florida is a long-ass drive from Missouri.

"I'm not ready to commit yet, Dad."

"You've been saying that for long enough. We're way past the hand-wringing now. If you don't commit, someone else will. We can't lose your spot."

"I need more time."

"For what?" he yells, his face reddening with anger. "Get your thumb out of your ass, Chase. We need to sign with Bama."

I sling my backpack over my shoulder and head toward my bedroom. "I've got lots of homework. Can we talk about this later?"

"I told the coach you're ready."

I sigh heavily and drop my head. "I'll be ready soon."

"You'll be ready when he comes here with your letter of intent."

I don't say anything else—it'll only antagonize him. Instead, I go to my room and sit down on my bed to work on my English paper. Or at least look like I am. My head's definitely not in it.

Most guys on my team would kill to have any of the schools after them that have offered me a full ride. They think I haven't committed because I'm playing hard to get.

My dad's right—it's past time. Coach Carter keeps telling me the same thing. But I'm too torn up over it. No place seems like the right one.

I take out my phone and text Gin.

Me: What are you doing?

Gin: Trying to cut plywood. It's harder than it looks.

Me: Huh, am I s'posed to ignore the hard wood jokes right now?

Gin: That would be good since I just cut my finger and I'm unlikely to laugh.

Me: You're not using a power saw or anything, are you? You can really hurt yourself with those.

Gin: Don't worry, all my digits are still attached . . . So what are you doing? Aren't you supposed to be at practice?

Me: It's over. And I'm trying to make a hard decision.

Gin: Blond, brunette, or redhead? I vote brunette.

I smile at the phone screen and almost laugh, which felt impossible five minutes ago.

Me: Naturally, bc you're a brunette . . .

Gin: No, I'm not. Brunette means brown. My hair is the color of the grim reaper's robe.

Me: Is death's robe bright red?

Gin: Shut up. You know what I mean.

Me: Why do you color your hair?

Gin: Because I like it this color.

Me: I don't believe you.

Gin: I don't care. Are we done here?

Me: No. When are we going out for pizza?

Gin: Can I text you later? I have to finish these cuts. The freshmen are all staring at me with open mouths and paintbrushes in their hand.

Me: Yeah. Don't forget.

Gin: I won't.

I toss my phone on the bed and try to focus on my paper. When my mom announces dinner's ready a few minutes later, I go into the kitchen and pick up my bowl and spoon from the table.

"Whoa, whoa," my dad says. "Sit down. We need to talk about Bama."

"I've got a paper to write, and then I have to watch film for the game. I have a thing after practice tomorrow, so this is the only night I can do it."

He lowers his brows, frustrated. I know the asshole well, though, so I know how to buy myself at least a few more days.

"Can you watch the film with me?" I ask him. "I could use some help analyzing their defense."

His brows shoot upward in surprise. "Sure. Just come find me when you're ready."

"Thanks."

I glance at my mom, who gives me a grateful look. I just saved her entire evening. Asking my dad for advice, which I rarely do, will mean he's in a good mood for a while.

It's fucking ridiculous that the only person in this house we have to tread carefully around is one of the adults. My sisters both have their heads down. They're focused on eating and getting the hell out of there, like I usually am.

I eat alone in my room, finish my paper, and then watch some film with my dad. He has a notebook and pen ready, and he takes notes as we watch and rewind the film.

If he weren't such a dick, I'd appreciate his enthusiasm. But I know none of this is about me. Not the film, not the college choice, not any of it. It's about him making me into the person he planned to be.

I'm in bed scrolling through social media when Gin finally texts at almost 10:00 p.m.

Gin: So did the brunette win out?

Me: It's a different decision, smartass.

Gin: Hmmm . . . what other decisions do football players make?

Me: You'd be surprised.

Gin: Anything I can help with?

Me: I don't know . . .

Gin: If it's pie or cake—pie. Bath or shower—bath. Bacon or any other food in the universe—bacon. Does that help?

Me: Helps me know I should ask you out for breakfast instead of pizza.

Gin: Ha.

Me: I'm trying to decide what school to go to.

Gin: I thought you had a full ride somewhere?

Me: I do, but there's more than one school to choose from.

Gin: I see.

Me: I know it's a "problem" most people would love to have . . .

Gin: No, it's a big decision. I get it.

Me: Do you know where you're going?

Gin: NYU.

Me: Wow, New York?

Gin: Yep.

Me: You didn't think about anywhere else?

Gin: No. I've always known it was NYU.

Me: I wish I knew where I'm supposed to go.

Gin: What schools are you thinking about?

Me: I like University of Iowa and Penn State. My dad likes Alabama and Ohio State.

Gin: You're the one who has to go there. You make the decision.

Me: I wish it were that simple.

Gin: It is.

Me: Did you get your wood cut?

Gin: I did. It only took about seven times longer than it takes the guy who usually cuts it for me.

Me: Hey, at least you did it.

Gin: I'm falling asleep . . .

Me: Go to bed, I'll see you tomorrow.

Gin: Okay. Bye.

I grin at her awkward signoff.

Me: Night, Gin.

thirteen

Gin

CLAY HOUSER HAS A SHIT-EATING grin as he walks up to our lunch table. He's got a towel thrown over one shoulder that looks like it came from one of the locker rooms.

My stomach churns at the thought of him tossing it at my face when it has God knows what all over it. It's been a quiet Thursday so far, with most people just ignoring me or giving me dirty looks.

"Asshole alert," Lauren says when Clay stops at our table.

Clay sneers at her. "What's it like for a dyke to suck dick for drugs? Bet you gag on 'em."

She laughs bitterly. "Curious about sucking dick, Clay? There are some videos online you can watch to learn."

Raj tries to muffle his laugh. Clay's cheeks darken with embarrassment.

"You bunch of freaks deserve each other," he mutters.

I put an arm out to shield my face as he starts to throw the towel, but it surprises all of us when he tosses it at Raj instead of me.

"Wrap it around your head, Osama," he sneers.

Several football players behind him are laughing it up. Raj is trying to ignore the whole thing, but the look on his face is gutting me.

Shame. Clay Houser made Raj feel ashamed of who he is, and it sparks my temper into an instant inferno. Raj doesn't say a mean word to anyone. His parents are dead, and the only reminder he gets of them at Roper High School is the taunting of rednecks.

I reach for the towel and get up from the table, advancing on Clay. I'm not even thinking; I'm just letting my white-hot rage guide my every move.

"Clay, I hope this towel is dirty."

There are only a few steps between me and him now, and he's giving me a bewildered look as I get closer. His cheering section has gone quiet.

"What are you doing?" he scoffs and looks from side to side.

My voice is ominously even. "I'm gonna shove this towel so far down your throat that you choke on it. I hope you taste ass and crotch as it goes down."

I throw myself at him then, rubbing the towel in his face. He seems too stunned to move for a few seconds, but then he grabs my shoulders and throws me off.

"Crazy bitch," he says under his breath.

I'm hurling myself at him for a second round when someone hooks an arm around my waist.

"Stop, Gin."

I turn to see the assistant principal, Mrs. Metz. I take a few deep breaths, and it sets in what I've done.

Shit. I'm probably getting a detention. It was worth it, though. After nearly a week of merciless tormenting over that stupid rose, I boiled over. Clay's treatment of Raj was just the last straw.

"To your office?" I ask Mrs. Metz.

She drops her hold on me. "I think that's a good idea."

I sulk the entire way to her office, sitting down and staying silent once we're inside.

"Gin, what's going on with you?" she asks, closing her office door.

Mrs. Metz seems okay. She's a Native American woman who married a Roper guy and now finds herself working at a Podunk school in the middle of nowhere. Still, I'm not apologizing for what I did to Clay. He deserved it—and much more.

I shrug. "Just the usual. Football players thinking they own the world around here."

She furrows her brow and sits down behind her desk. "How so?"

"Did you see what happened?"

"I just saw you lunging at Clay, and that's so unlike you. There must have been a reason."

"Yeah, he threw a towel at Raj and said something about him putting it on his head."

Mrs. Metz's expression darkens.

"Roper's finest," I say, rolling my eyes.

"Gin, I agree with you that Clay's behavior was unacceptable, and I will address it. But you know your response wasn't okay either."

"I'm tired of it." I hold her gaze across her desk. "Football players get anything they want. They make derogatory, sexist, racist comments and everyone chalks it up to 'our boys blowing off steam.'" I emphasize my words with air quotes.

"When those comments happen, you need to report them."

I shake my head. "That's a lot of reporting. And then what?

They'll get in trouble? No. They'll get a slap on the wrist from you and a pat on the ass from their piece-of-shit coach."

"Gin."

I cross my arms and narrow my eyes. "I know you have to talk the talk, Mrs. Metz. Tell me what I did was wrong. But you know I'm right. And I'm not sorry for what I did. Clay's a disgusting pig. Raj is my friend. He doesn't stand up for himself, but I won't just sit there while he gets treated that way. I wouldn't let *anyone* be treated that way."

Mrs. Metz nods curtly. "Just head for your next class, okay? I'll handle Clay."

"Do I have detention? Are you calling my mom?"

She shakes her head.

"I don't mind if you call my mom. Just know that she may break into applause," I say. "She might order me a cake for tonight that says, 'Way to go, Gin.'"

Mrs. Metz is trying not to smile. "Go to class. If anyone asks, I *talked the talk*, okay?"

"Yeah." I stand up and sling my backpack over my shoulder. "And I listened."

Once again, everyone's talking about me. All afternoon, people whisper and stare when I walk into a room or when I'm in the hallways. Apparently, they're saying I tried to start a fight with Clay, and he refused to fight me.

He's a real gentleman, that Clay.

I make it to the end of the school day, feeling lighter as I walk backstage in the theater. I'm working on creating abstract castle spires with my crew, and it's not easy. We had to throw out our first attempt, which looked like tie-dyed lollipops.

My crew of three freshmen boys and one sophomore girl are all staring at me in wide-eyed silence.

"You guys, it was no big deal," I tell them. "I didn't fight anyone. Let's get to work on Castle Spires 2.0, okay?"

I lean the pieces of plywood I cut yesterday up against some five-gallon paint buckets, then pass out brushes and get them going on painting the spires dark gray, which will be their base color. I'm on my knees, stirring paints to be used as accent shades when a deep voice sounds behind me.

"Reporting for duty, boss."

I stop stirring, the hairs on the back of my neck standing on end. It's Chase, but what is he doing here? I turn and give him a confused look.

"Why aren't you at practice?"

"I'm on my way there. But when I'm done, I'm volunteering here."

"Here as in . . . ?"

He grins and points at the spires. "I'll be helping you with . . . whatever that is."

I lower my brows in frustration. "They're castle spires."

"Yeah, I figured." His cocky grin widens, and he winks at me.

My face warms against my will. I clear my throat and return to stirring, forcing myself to look impassive.

"Okay, well . . . wear old clothes you don't mind getting paint on."

He nods and walks closer to me. "Okay. I'll be here by five."

I look up at him. "We'll be waiting with bated breath."

Another grin from him and another somersault in my stomach. I want to focus on the paint I'm stirring, but he's holding my gaze, and I can't make myself stop staring into his faded denim-blue eyes.

"See you soon, Gin."

He hooks the second strap of his backpack over his arm and

shrugs it all the way on, then walks away. I still can't stop staring. I watch as he jogs down the stairs on the side of the stage.

Madison stops in the middle of the scene she's rehearsing to say something to him. I don't hear what it is because I'm entirely focused on Chase, but he smiles and nods at her before heading out an auditorium door.

One of the freshmen clears his throat. My attention snaps toward him, and he snickers.

"You need something?" I ask, my tone agitated.

He shakes his head. "You just looked distracted."

"Just paint, would you? We're behind schedule since we had to trash the first set of spires."

"What are we doing with these? They aren't abstract. Aren't they supposed to be abstract?"

I narrow my eyes at him. "We're getting there, Skippy. First, they need a base coat of gray."

Returning to the paint I'm stirring, I take a deep breath and try to think about anything but Chase. He had to have heard that I jumped one of his teammates at lunch today and tried to stuff a towel in his mouth. But still, he showed up here with that flirty grin.

And why is he volunteering here? I've never seen Chase volunteer for any team or activity. The drama club often gets stuck with Jack Pearson, the loudest a-hole imaginable.

It has to be about me. I know that, and it makes my heart pound and my blood race with nervous energy. Chase is still trying to persuade me to give it up to the Roper High football team, and even though there's a zero percent chance that will happen, I don't mind his attention.

I *pretend* I mind, but deep down, I like that he texts me. My senior year is nothing like I expected it would be, but that's been the one bright spot. Chase Matthews finally actually *sees* me. And when he looks at me, emotions flicker in his eyes. Sure, they range from pissed off to confounded to amused, but the point is—they're *feelings*. I never thought we'd even have a conversation, and now we've had several.

From now on, though, I have to watch myself. No one can know I secretly like him. God, that would be humiliating. I just got busted by a freshman getting googly-eyed, and that's very un-Gin-ish.

I'm cool AF. Calm AF. Collected AF.

I finish stirring the red paint and move on to shaking the can of purple.

He's probably volunteering here so he can make a last-ditch effort to convince me to be his tribute tomorrow night. His plan was likely to get friendly with me during the week so I let down my guard and then make me feel like it would mean something to him if we had sex.

It's not happening. He'll have to give another girl a rose in the morning, and he'll be screwing her tomorrow night.

The thought turns the churning warmth in my belly into a pile of smoldering ash.

~

AS PROMISED, CHASE SHOWS UP backstage just before 5:00 p.m. His hair is damp like he just took a shower. When he's a few feet away, I get a hint of a soapy smell that confirms he did.

Be cool, Gin.

"Hey," he says in greeting.

"Hi." I point to the brushes and paint I set out for him. "You can start with those. We need all those boards painted green. They're going to be grass for our outdoor set."

He nods and arches a brow playfully. "You don't trust me with anything harder than grass?"

"Let's see how you do with that first." I give him a half smile.

After walking to the other side of the set building area, he looks back at me. I put him on the opposite end of me deliberately, so the freshmen are between us. I don't need anyone else noticing how hard it is for me not to pay attention to anything but Chase when he's around.

I'm working with Lane, one of the freshmen boys, on our abstract castle spires. No matter what we do, they won't be Broadway quality, because they're made of freaking plywood, but we're doing our best. We're trying to make them look like they're from Van Gogh's *Starry Night*.

"Like this?" Lane asks me, swirling his brush through the wet paint.

"Yeah, that's good."

As always, I'm listening to the rehearsal with one ear. It's hard not to follow along and learn all the lines when you hear them repeated so many times.

"Sometimes it's overwhelming being a prince," Aiden, who plays Prince Charming, says. "I wish I could just say what I'm really thinking sometimes, you know?"

There's a long pause before Madison says, "You . . . uh, I mean . . . you can?"

I turn my head to the side and feed her the next line in a loud whisper. "Can't you? You're the only one here who definitely won't get beheaded for having an opinion."

She repeats the line, and Aiden moves on with his part of the scene. I think Madison learned the first act of the play, but she struggles with the second and third acts. And her understudy, Grace, doesn't seem to know *any* of it. She should be the one helping Madison remember lines, not me.

Hopefully by our opening night in a month, Madison will know the script by heart. Otherwise, it'll be pretty painful to watch.

Lane and I finish our spires, and they look much better than our first attempt did. It's approaching 6:00 p.m., and everyone's packing up to leave.

"Need help cleaning up?" Chase asks me.

I glance up at him. "I'll get it when I'm done, thanks. Great job on the grass."

He shrugs. "It was kind of hard to mess up." He runs a hand through his hair, now dry and back to its usual dark gold shade. "You're not leaving?"

"I have a few things to finish up. I have to teach lessons at the Y at seven, and there's not really enough time for me to go home in between."

Our eyes lock, a silent spark of electricity passing between us. Is he thinking about seeing me at the Y the other night, or is that just me?

"I'll stay and help," he offers.

"No, you don't have to. I don't mind."

"I know, I just—"

"I'm not having sex with you," I blurt.

Lane widens his eyes and walks away. Chase gives me a sheepish grin.

"I don't expect you to, Gin. I'm just offering my help with the painting."

My cheeks warm with embarrassment. Where did that outburst come from?

"I know, but if you're trying to make nice so you can bring me a rose again tomorrow . . . please don't. *Please*. It'll be another no. It'll always be a no."

Chase's expression sobers. "I know. That's not why I'm here."

"Then . . . why *are* you here?"

"Yeah, why are you here?" Madison barges in between us, addressing Chase. "And what are you doing after? Want to get something to eat?"

"No, I'm not leaving yet."

Madison looks at Chase, who is looking at me. She turns to me, then back to him, with a confused look.

"Ooookay," she says, shrugging.

She leaves, and slowly, everyone else trickles out of the theater too. Soon it's just Chase and me.

The bright stage lights illuminate the empty stage, so I switch them off.

"If you want to help, we can paint this last spire," I say, passing him the brush Lane was using.

He bends to dip his brush in the paint, turning to me. "I'm sorry about what happened with Clay at lunch today."

"It's nothing new. Why be sorry now?"

"I've never condoned that kind of shit."

I press my lips together, willing myself not to speak, but I can't help it. I'm made to fire back.

"So gangbanging is okay, but racist jokes aren't. Got it."

Chase sighs softly. "Come on, Gin. I thought we kind of had a truce happening."

"Is it over?" I set my brush down on the tarp and stand up, crossing my arms and looking down at him. "This whole me being one of the Sweet Sixteen thing, I mean. Are you guys going to ask me again or . . . I don't know, jump me behind the school one day?"

He stands up, contrition on his face. "No. I'd never let that happen. I'm not as bad a guy as you seem to think."

The aggravation in his tone makes me roll my eyes.

"Really? Because I think you lead a group of guys who gang-bang a new girl every Friday night of the football season."

Our eyes stay locked as several seconds of silence pass.

"Clay is benched for tomorrow night's entire game," he finally says.

"Whose decision was that? Your coach usually doesn't give a rat's ass how you guys treat others."

Chase looks at the ceiling, locks his hands behind his head and laughs.

"Gin Fielding, you're not like any other girl I've ever met. You drive me crazy half the time and ride my ass the rest of the time. And you say things like *rat's ass*."

My heart pounds as I make myself look dismissive. "I didn't ask you to come here. And I don't want to be like other girls."

Chase puts his hands on his hips, his eyes on me. "I came here because I wanted to. I like that you aren't like other girls. And it was *me* who made the decision for Clay to get benched."

I'm taken aback. "You?"

"Coach would rather have me on the field than Clay."

"He had to choose?"

Chase shrugs and looks out over the empty theater chairs. "I told him if it came to it, he'd have to."

"Well, that's . . ." I swallow, searching for words. "Thanks, I think. Clay's really gonna have it out for me now, though."

"No, he won't. I took care of it. He won't bother you again. Or Lauren and Raj."

I exhale deeply. "Okay. Thanks. Though I wouldn't have this problem if you hadn't tried to give me that damn rose last Friday. What were you thinking, giving it to me?"

A slight smile plays on his lips. "If I could do it over again, I wouldn't. And like I said, I'm sorry. Can we move on? Maybe . . . be friends?"

"I guess so. But my first order of business as your friend is to tell you that you seriously need to rethink this whole Sweet Sixteen thing."

"It wasn't my idea, Gin. This has been going on for years. Since the 90s, I think."

"So what?"

He bends back down and picks up his paintbrush. "Are we gonna work on this spire?"

I glance over at the digital clock backstage. "We should clean up, actually. I need to get to the Y so I can get changed."

We clean the brushes and seal up the paint cans. When we're about to head out, I give Chase a heads-up about the streak of green paint on his cheek.

Oh, to be one of those girls who reaches over to wipe it off for him. I'm so not, though.

"Do you, uh . . . want a ride?" I ask Chase as we walk out the side door.

"Yeah, thanks."

He barely fits in my passenger seat with his large frame. I don't bother asking where he lives, because in Roper, everyone knows where everyone lives.

When I pull into the driveway of his house, he reaches for the door handle and then looks over at me.

"Text me when you get home later. Since we're friends now."

With that, he winks at me and gets out of my car.

I should really roll my eyes and make a comment under my breath. But I can't.

My principles tell me to despise Chase Matthews, but my

crush on him won't allow it. So for now, I'll have to stay in this weird in-between place.

Because while I secretly like him—*a lot*—I know what tomorrow morning is. It's rose day.

No matter how Chase makes me feel, he's part of something I find sickening. Even my crush isn't strong enough to overcome how I feel about that.

fourteen

Chase

MY THIRTY-YARD THROW TO JACK is perfect. He catches it and covers the short distance to the end zone, adding another cherry on top of our 39–12 victory.

The crowd is cheering and the guys are celebrating, but I feel like I'm not completely here right now. I played tonight's game on autopilot, making the throws and running the plays that have become second nature to me.

My head's been elsewhere all day. When I gave Sophie Chambers a rose this morning, I smiled and she smiled as what felt like the whole school looked on. They seemed to breathe a collective sigh of relief that things are back to normal now.

They all knew we'd win tonight. They all knew Sophie was the one we'd decided as a team was hot enough to celebrate with us tonight. And while that all felt slightly wrong this morning, I chalked it up to my mojo being off from Gin saying no last week. To maybe being a little bit over high school football in general.

Ready to move on to a bigger game, where I have to bust my ass just to hold my spot on the team.

But then I saw Michelle Zimmerman. She's a senior, like me, and today was her first day back at school after a thirty-day stay at rehab. Everyone knew her drinking had gotten worse the past several months, and that she was dabbling in some pretty hard drugs.

None of us had guessed she'd try to kill herself, though. Her mom had found her in bed with an empty pill bottle on the floor, and she'd had to get drugs pumped out of her stomach and then she'd been admitted to rehab.

And now, she's back, but one look at her told me she's not the same girl we all knew before. She's thinner, to the point of looking frail. Her long blond hair is cut to shoulder length now and pulled back in a ponytail at the nape of her neck. And even though it's still warm enough for shorts and T-shirts this mid-September, she's wearing pants and a baggy shirt with long sleeves.

I never knew Michelle well. It set in when I was thinking that, how weird it is to say that about someone I've had sex with, but it's true. She was one of the Sweet Sixteen last year.

She enjoyed it. They all do. But when I saw her this morning—when she saw me looking at her from across the hall and her eyes locked on mine, I almost stumbled back from the wave of emotion I felt coming off of her.

Was she just calling me out for looking at her, like everyone else is today? Or was she trying to tell me something? It wasn't a kind look. It was more like she was telling me she's stripped bare now, all the way down to the bone. More naked than she was that drunken night last year. And that I'm more a part of what's happened to her since than I want to admit.

"Hey, you need a ride to the cabin?" Jack asks me as we walk to the locker room after the game.

"Nah. I actually think I pulled my groin."

"Shit, how?"

I shrug. "No idea."

"You're not pussing out on the party. Put some ice on your crotch and drink a few beers, you'll be good."

I nod, just to get him off my back. My groin is fine, but I thought up the lie earlier so I won't have to explain why I'm not fucking Sophie.

I wasn't feeling it anyway, but after the way Michelle looked at me earlier, it's not an option. I can't even think straight—much less think about sex—until I figure things out.

What I really want is to talk things over with Gin. Her unfiltered honesty is what I need, and I trust her. That'll have to wait, though. There are a couple other things I have to do first, or I won't be able to sleep tonight.

After a quick shower, I dress and head for the concession stand. My dad's there in his usual spot, breaking down the game with friends at a picnic table. His eyes light up when he sees me.

"Good game, son." He stands and claps me on the shoulder.

I smile and thank him, though the words taste bitter. He never calls me "son" unless we're around other people.

"Hey, can I borrow your truck?" I ask him.

He fishes for the keys in the pocket of his jeans and passes them to me. "You got it. Have a good time."

I could've asked him if I could commit murder, and he would have smiled and said yes. As long as we get the win, nothing else matters.

Nothing. And that's why my stomach's been churning all damn day.

I thank my dad, and he tells me where to find the truck. I get stopped several times on the way to the parking lot by people who want to congratulate me or ask me about the game. One of those times, it's my sister Cassie who stops me.

"Hey, Dad said you're taking his truck. Are you going to the party? Can I come with you?"

"No." I say it more forcefully than I meant to.

Cassie crosses her arms and cocks her head. "Why not? I'm old enough."

"No, you're not. Go home, Cass. Or go get pizza with your friends. You're not going to the party."

"Come on, Chase. Please?"

"Look, that's not even where I'm going. I'll give you a ride somewhere else if you want."

She considers. "Okay, let me tell my friends."

I assume she means tell them she's leaving with me, but instead, I find myself in the truck with Cassie and three of her giggling sophomore friends. One of them rolls down the passenger side window on the way out of the parking lot, and they all wave and call out to people.

I wish I felt a shred of their energy. Instead, I feel beat down. It's partly physical from the game, but mostly mental.

The whole way to the girl's house I'm taking them to, I grip the steering wheel hard, questions racing through my mind. After dropping them off, I make the ten-minute drive to Michelle's, parking on the street in front of her family's two-story brick home on a tree-lined street.

It's a quiet neighborhood with nice sidewalks—a notch above the average Roper one. I'm halfway up the sidewalk leading to the front door when I stop.

I shouldn't have come here. It was her first day back at school, and she's been through a lot. I'm not even a friend of hers.

But something makes me keep walking. I need an answer to the question that's been bothering me since seeing her in the hallway this morning.

The lights are still on in the living room, so I knock softly at the front door. After a minute or so, a man with graying hair opens the door, giving me a puzzled look.

"Can I help you?" he asks.

"I'm sorry for coming by so late, sir. I was wondering if Michelle is here."

He furrows his brow and then shakes his head.

"I'm sorry, she's—"

"It's okay, Dad." Michelle approaches from behind him.

He looks at her skeptically, concern etched on his face.

"It's okay," she says again.

He steps aside, and Michelle looks at me.

"What are you doing here, Chase?"

I sigh softly. What *am* I doing here? I'm supposed to be on the way to the party, to drink away my troubles.

"Can we talk for a minute?" I ask.

Her dad opens his mouth to protest, so I add, "Just sitting on the front step, maybe?"

"Yeah." Michelle gives her dad a weak smile of reassurance and then steps outside, closing the door behind her.

She sits down first, and when I join her, I make sure to leave a foot of space between us. I don't want to make her feel uncomfortable. That's an odd thought to have, though, given our history.

"I'm glad you're back," I say. "How was the first day?"

She shrugs. "About as expected. Lots of staring and whispering. People trying to get a look at my wrists to see if there are slash marks, even though I used pills."

A few moments of awkward silence hang in the cool night air.

"What are you doing here?" Michelle asks again. "Aren't you supposed to be at the party?"

"I need to ask you something. I don't know if I'm a dick for coming over here on your first day back and bringing up something that might make you feel bad, but—"

Her laugh is humorless. "I've spent the past thirty days talking for hours every day about stuff that makes me feel bad. I've gotten pretty good at it."

I take a deep breath and go for it. "Did the Sweet Sixteen thing have anything to do with . . . what happened?"

Michelle arches her brows in surprise. "With my suicide attempt, you mean?"

"Yeah."

Her exhale sounds heavy. "Look, I'm just trying to get by at school. I don't need anyone getting pissed off at me. I missed a month of schoolwork, and I'm really behind."

"This will stay between us. No one will even know I came over here, you have my word. I just need to know for myself."

There's another silence, but this one doesn't feel quite as uncomfortable. I pick up a rock from the flower bed next to the front step, rubbing my thumb over its smooth surface as I wait.

After a little while, Michelle responds.

"I guess that was kind of the beginning for me. When you gave me that rose, I felt . . . I don't know, validated. Other girls were jealous. I've always been skinny, and I'll never have the curves I wish I did. But when the time came, doing it . . . I guess it felt like the price I needed to pay for popularity. The only socially acceptable answer was yes. Saying no . . . wasn't even an option. And after it was over, I drank for the first time. I overdid it and got so sick. But that became my solution. Something bad happens, or things get overwhelming—just drink it away. Then I got introduced to drugs. They were cheaper and easier than booze for me. And saying no never felt like an option to me. I see now that it was, though." She blows out a breath and turns to me. "I don't know, did that answer your question?"

I swallow, staring across her front yard at the glowing lamp on the post. "You didn't . . . enjoy it, then?"

Her eyes bulge, and she shakes her head. "I mean, I don't want to offend you or anything, but . . . no. I was *terrified*. Everyone was seeing me naked, and I knew it was going to hurt, and . . . like I said, I saw it as a price to be paid. A ticket into a club that would make me popular. So other girls would envy me."

I turn toward the flower bed, a wave of nausea making me want to bend over and throw up. I take a few deep breaths to steady myself.

When I turn back to face Michelle, I say, "I know it's not worth much, but I'm sorry. If I had known—"

She gives me a pitying smile. "You had to know. Those parties aren't for the girls, Chase. They're for the football team. Do you really think any girl could honestly enjoy *that*? Why do you think they're usually drunk before it even starts?"

I shake my head. "I guess I'm a fucking idiot. I've just said what all the guys who were older than me said when I was a freshman playing football. It's consensual, they can change their minds . . ."

"Oh my God." Michelle wraps her arms around herself. "What would happen to a girl who changed her mind, though?"

"I'll never do it again." I look into her eyes, hoping she can feel my sincerity. "I'm sorry I was such a stupid asshole."

Michelle's expression softens. "It wasn't just that, Chase. I made a series of really bad decisions that led to my suicide attempt."

"I know, but . . . it's not right. That's what I'm hearing from you. It made you feel . . ."

"Gross," she finishes for me. "Your first time being with twelve guys—or however many it was—is gross. When we talked about it in rehab, I realized someday when I have a boyfriend from somewhere else, I'll have to tell him about it."

"The right kind of guy won't blame you for it."

"I hope. But I'm also a recovering addict, and I attempted suicide. I've got lots of baggage."

"You're a survivor. You've got nothing to be ashamed of. I can't say the same."

She rubs her hands up and down her arms. I wish I had a hoodie to offer her, but I'm just wearing my dress shirt from after the game.

"You're the first person to talk to me today. Other than teachers and my parents, I mean. I ate my lunch alone in my car. So . . . thanks, I guess."

"Keep your chin up. It'll get better. And I know this is awkward as fuck, but if you ever need a friend . . . to talk or whatever, call me."

"Thanks." She turns back to look at her front door. "I should get inside. My parents worry about me every second now."

I feel an urge to apologize to her, but I already did that—twice—so I just stand up and say nothing.

"See you at school," she says.

"See you."

I walk back to the truck in a daze, just sitting there for a full minute after I get in without starting it.

I'm an asshole. All my life, I've sworn I wouldn't turn out like my dad, and I just found out that, like him, I'm a complete asshole. I don't even know what to do with the realization.

When I start up the truck and put it in drive, I know there's no way I'm going to that party. I've done more than enough damage already.

I can't even text Gin tonight. If I tell her I see now what she's been saying all along about the Sweet Sixteen, her *I told you so's* might make me actually throw up. I'm already on the edge of it.

Instead, I drive home. As I park in the driveway, I hope to hell my old man's out drinking with his buddies because I can't even stand to look at him right now.

Turns out I'm a chip off the old block I hate so much.

fifteen

Gin

WHEN I WALK INTO PLAY practice after school Monday, I give Chase's green "grass" a scowl. I saw him at lunch earlier and should have scowled then, but he acted like he didn't even know me.

I know there's nothing between us, but I'd gotten used to his nightly texts. When we passed in the hallway, he'd started give me a look that felt loaded with secret meaning.

But then he ignored me all weekend. Not one text. It's stupid for me to be acting like a scorned girlfriend—I knew when I saw him give Sophie a rose Friday morning that Chase was never really into me.

Would I have really wanted him to text me in the middle of the night Friday, drunk, after having sex with Sophie?

No. I'm constantly fighting the knowledge that the fantasy Chase I've had a crush on since hitting puberty doesn't really exist. He's slept with so many girls that he for sure qualifies as a man whore.

I'm uptight; he's outgoing. I have two friends, and he has two hundred. I'm an artist, and he's an athlete. I hate Roper High School and everything it stands for, and he's pretty much the poster boy for it.

I tell my painting crew to come up with a plan for a streetlamp and get started on it, then I put in my earbuds and get lost in the wall of lockers I'm painting on a sheet of plywood.

It's nice that this project requires no creativity. Once I've gotten the style down for one locker, I just repeat it and work my way down the line. It lets me stay lost in the thoughts in my head.

I'll never be like Chase. I may not be an experienced sex goddess, but when I do have sex, it'll mean something. People treat sex like entertainment, and I don't get it. It's the most intimate thing you can do with another person.

Given all the girls Chase has slept with, sex can't be much more than a transaction for him. Not that I ever wanted to sleep with him, I just wanted him to notice me. Talk to me. And he did, so I got what I wanted. It's time to move on.

I'm on the second to last locker when a tap on my shoulder makes me turn around, taking out an earbud as I do.

"Hi, boss," Chase says from behind me. "Need to me paint you some more grass?"

My mouth falls open with surprise as I look up at him.

Words, Gin. Say some words.

"Uh . . . yeah. I mean . . . what are you doing here?"

A corner of his mouth turns up slightly in a grin. "I'm your volunteer, remember?"

"Yeah, but today too?"

He nods. "Every day. You said you're behind, so what can I do?"

"Um . . ." I shake my head, trying to think. "I need to assemble some sets, if you want to help with that."

"Sure."

"Okay, just let me finish this, and then we'll do it."

I look away from him, trying to appear indifferent. My heart is racing, but he doesn't know that.

"Hey," he says in a soft tone, leaning in to speak in my ear. "I'm sorry I've been quiet. I had some thinking to do."

"Don't you mean *fucking*?" I turn to look up at him, my brows arched.

He shakes his head. "I didn't go Friday night."

"Why not?"

He looks over at the freshmen painting their lamppost, who are all trying to appear immersed in their work.

"Can we talk about this when we're alone?" Chase asks me.

"Yeah, sure."

He has the damp hair and soapy scent again, and it's impossible not to be distracted by it. When I'm running low on paint, he pours more into my tray for me, but other than that, he stands next to me in silence until people start filing out of play practice.

"Do you know where the shop room is?" I ask him.

"Yeah."

I walk over to the wall and take a key from a peg there. "This is the key. Can you go in there and get us some hammers and nails?"

"Sure. What size nails?"

I give him a blank look, then hold out my thumb and index finger to show him the length I think we'll need to build the sets. He grins and takes the key.

My crew of underclassmen all leave while he's gone. Everyone else is heading out too, when Madison approaches me, a confused look on her face.

"What's Chase doing hanging out with you?"

"We're not hanging out, we're building sets."

"Yeah, but . . . why?"

"For the play. So you guys aren't standing on an empty stage."

She gives me an exasperated sigh and puts a hand on her hip. "You know what I mean. Why is he helping you?"

"I guess you'd have to ask him that." I shrug and put my earbud back in, dismissing her.

I finish up the lockers, and I'm at the backstage sink washing out brushes when Chase returns, two hammers in one hand and a plastic container of nails in the other.

"So?" I look over at him.

"So?"

"So what were you thinking about all weekend?"

His expression turns from relaxed to serious, and he runs a hand through his hair.

"A lot of things. I realized that you're right about . . . stuff. And also that you're way too good for me."

It feels like every ounce of blood in my body rushes to my head at once. "What? Too good for me? You, I mean?"

He nods and walks closer to the sink, speaking in a low tone even though we're alone.

"I get it, Gin. Why you said no. Why you were right to. And I admire you for it."

I switch off the water faucet. "Why the sudden change of heart?"

"It wasn't completely sudden. I'd started to . . . wonder, I guess."

"Did something happen to Sophie Friday night?"

He shakes his head. "I don't know, I wasn't there."

I tear off a paper towel and dry my hands. "Chase, are you okay? And what do you mean about me being too good for you?

Aren't we just friends?"

He sets the hammer and nails down on a table and leans back against its edge.

"I hope we're friends, but I don't feel like I even deserve that at this point."

"Why not?"

"Because I'm everything you said I was. Captain of a team of guys who . . ." He cringes and looks away. "I'm ashamed of what I've done. What we've *all* done on my watch."

I'm so floored by his turnaround that I'm not even sure what to say. I let a few seconds pass before I speak again.

"So then . . . what are you going to do?"

He scrubs his hands over his face. "That's what I spent the weekend thinking about. And I don't know. I can't do it anymore, I know that."

"Can't do what?"

"The Sweet Sixteen. I'll never give out another rose, and I'll never go to that party again."

He crosses his arms over his chest. I just look at him. It's one of the few times that a response doesn't fly out of my mouth before I even think about it. Chase has left me stunned speechless.

"Well . . . that's a big decision," I finally manage. "You may want to sleep on it a few more nights."

"No, I'm sure. It's the right decision, don't you think?"

"I do, but . . . it won't be easy."

"I know that. And, Gin, I also decided I'm not playing any more games. Not with anyone, not ever. So I'm telling you straight up that I like you—a lot. Not just as a friend. But like I said, you're way out of my league."

I laugh at that. *"I'm* out of *your* league?"

Chase nods seriously. "You're smart and brave and

compassionate. I'm none of those things."

"I don't know about that. Maybe you're a work in progress."

He scoffs and smiles. "I've got a long way to go, then."

"You still look like you have the weight of the world on your shoulders."

"It's a lot to process."

"And you aren't going to tell me what prompted this epiphany?"

"I'll tell you that it started with you. And that without you, it never would have happened."

Again, I'm floored. Chase doesn't just *see* me now; he's actually listening to me too. It's an overwhelming, heady sensation.

"So I have an idea," I say. "Why don't we leave the set building for another day, and instead we can go to my house and have dinner with my mom. I think she's making lasagna tonight."

"You don't have to teach swim lessons tonight?"

"No. I mean, if you're not hungry or you already have—"

"I'm starving, and I'd love to."

I tuck my hair behind both ears and smile. "Good. She makes great lasagna. And, Chase, I'm not too good to be your friend."

"Would you have liked me as more? If I wasn't such an irredeemable douchebag?"

"I don't know."

His face falls, and I feel like this may be the funniest, most ironic moment of my life.

"Maybe," I say, shrugging. "Probably."

He takes a step closer, turning an ear toward me. "Keep going . . ."

I roll my eyes. "You know the answer to this. Yes. Obviously, yes."

"I didn't know. You're pretty tough to read."

"Well . . . now you know." I walk over to my backpack and pick it up from the ground, sliding it on. "Ready to go, douchebag?"

"Ah, shit. You're gonna start calling me that now, aren't you?"

"I'm sure you've been called worse. And if not, you're gonna be soon."

He shakes his head and sighs. "Don't remind me. Tonight, let's just hang out and eat lasagna."

I turn off the stage lights, and we leave the darkened theater together.

Sixteen

Chase

THE BRICK MANSION GIN LIVES in is the nicest house in town. Nothing else even comes close. It doesn't really fit in Roper, and the way it sits alone on top of a hill, secluded by trees, it's like the house knows that.

As Gin drives up the long driveway, I get my first good look in a long time at the front of the place. Only the back is visible from the road. There are big concrete planters loaded with brightly colored flowers and tall, wood, double front doors.

The garage and carriage house are bigger than my family's entire home. The place is more like an estate than just a house, with landscaping as far as I can see on one side. There's a guy in jeans trimming hedges over there.

"I remember coming to your birthday party here when we were kids," I say. "Coolest party ever."

"My mom used to love having people over." Gin parks her car and turns it off, glancing over at me.

"She doesn't anymore?"

She shrugs. "I guess not as much, no. She stopped opening it for the Christmas Walk after she overheard some people talking about us. She said that wasn't the reason why, but I think it was."

"What did they say?"

"The usual. That she was wrong for bringing me into the world without a father, that her books are awful and she has to be a psychopath to write that stuff, and that we're Communists."

I laugh, thinking she's joking, but she arches her brows and stares me down.

"You think I'm kidding?"

My smile fades. "Well . . . about the communist part . . . yeah."

"No, that happened. My mom donates to Planned Parenthood, and they were saying she's too liberal for Roper."

I scoff at that. "More like too successful. You guys can't let assholes get to you."

"I agree. But she's sensitive to comments about me not having a father."

"You have one, though, right? You just don't know him?"

"Right. And I'm more than okay with it."

"Wish I didn't know mine," I mumble.

"Why?"

"Never mind." I clear my throat. "You sure your mom won't mind me coming?"

Gin smiles. "Not at all. I texted her when we were on the way to my car. She said the lasagna is already in the oven."

"Sounds amazing. That cafeteria cheeseburger I had at lunch today was like a hockey puck."

"Eww." I wrinkle my nose at the image.

"Yeah. Hard, burned, and cold. Couldn't even finish it, and I eat just about anything."

Gin opens her car door, and I follow. She gets her backpack out of the backseat, but I leave mine since she'll be taking me home later.

"Hey, Gin," the guy trimming the bushes calls out.

He sets down the shears and walks toward us. He's a tall, fit-looking guy with salt-and-pepper hair and a friendly smile.

"Hi, Michael," Gin says. "How's it going?"

He looks up at the sky and grins. "Sun's shining. I can't complain."

"This is my friend Chase Matthews," she says.

He holds his hand out to shake mine.

"Nice to meet you, Chase."

Gin shoulders her backpack and starts walking toward the back of the house.

"Dinner will be on soon, I think," she calls to Michael over her shoulder. "Lasagna."

"I smelled it cooking when I was polishing the banister earlier." He pats his stomach and chuckles, heading back for the shears.

"Nice guy," I say to Gin. "Is he a relative?"

"He works here, taking care of the place. It's a lot to keep up with, so he does it full time."

I nod. "Cool. Looks like he does a great job. The yard looks like it belongs in some magazine."

She pauses outside of a simple door with planters on either side. "My mom makes a lot of money, but she's not an asshole about it. She gives a lot to charity. People in Roper—"

I stop her, putting my hand over hers, which is hovering over the doorknob. "Hey. I don't think she's an asshole at all. She raised you, and you're about the nicest person I've ever met. Just because my family doesn't have money doesn't mean I judge people who do."

Gin's smile is wide. "You think I'm nice? Even though every other word out of my mouth is profane? Even though I tried to cram a towel down your teammate's throat today?"

"Yeah. You're not nice in a generic sense. You're nice in the ways that are hard but matter the most. You stand up for people." I pause, thinking of Michelle. "You care about people in a way . . . I admire, I guess is the best way to say it. That's why I don't deserve you, and no other guy in this town does either."

I said more than I meant to. There're a couple feet of space between us, but as I look into her blue eyes, she feels too close. Close enough to reach out and touch.

I don't care about her goth-looking black hair or her boring, sensible clothes. For the first time in my life, I'm attracted to a girl because of everything she is that has nothing to do with her looks.

Gin's attractive, sure—I picture her body, dripping wet in that swimsuit—many times a day, but that's not what keeps me up at night thinking about her. It's the things she says. The things she does. Her witty texts. The way she feeds Madison lines when she forgets them at play practice. Her infectious laugh, which sounds like music because it's hard to earn. Her fearless defense of anyone being picked on.

Gin puts up with no bullshit, and I find that unbelievably sexy.

She's perfectly still, looking like she's not even breathing as we stand there with our eyes locked on each other. I take a step closer to her, wanting to feel her warmth. She inhales sharply but doesn't move.

I'd love to be more than friends with Gin, but after what I've done, I can't. She'll just have to be a friend I can't get enough of.

I move a little closer, and her blue eyes widen. She still doesn't seem to be inhaling or exhaling. No matter how close I get, I feel an urge to go just a little further.

The doorknob turns from the other side, and Gin jumps, the spell broken. Her mom opens the door and smiles at us.

"Oh, hi. Didn't mean to scare you. I was just coming out to tell Michael dinner's almost ready."

"I told him," Gin says. She turns to me and says, "Mom, you remember Chase?"

"Of course. I'm so glad you're here, Chase. Call me Julia. I hope you're hungry. Come on in, guys."

She leads the way, and Gin lags behind her, leaning in to say something in a low tone when her mom's out of earshot.

"Don't worry, she's not gonna judge you over the Sweet Sixteen thing."

My heart starts beating triple time. "What? She knows about that?"

"She's not like other moms. It's cool."

I stop, glaring down at her. "It's *not* cool. Dammit, Gin. She knows I . . . oh, man."

I cover my face with both hands. Gin puts a palm on my back, pushing me forward.

"It's not a big deal, honest," she says.

Easy for her to say.

I exhale deeply and shoot her a dirty look as we walk through a big room with lots of windows, potted plants, and books lining shelves. We continue through the massive, wood-floored house, and I can't help admiring it as we go. The house is old, but it's so well-cared for and warm that it doesn't feel old at all. There are comfortable-looking couches and chairs and thick throw rugs on the floors.

"So how was school?" Julia asks as we walk into the massive, open kitchen.

"Um . . ." Gin's gaze falls on a vase of bright pink roses on the island. She gasps and presses a palm to her chest. "Oh shit! It's your birthday!"

Julia smiles and waves a hand. "When you get to be my age, it's not a big deal."

"Who sent the flowers?" Gin leans closer to smell one. "Are they from your editor?"

"Uh . . . no, those are from Michael, actually."

Gin arches her brows and grins. "Oh really?"

"Hush," Julia says, her face flushing. "He just remembered how much I love it when the rose bush with pink flowers is in bloom in the yard, so he ordered these."

"Uh-huh." Gin turns to me and waggles her brows. "Mom's got a boyfriend."

"I do not!" Julia rolls her eyes. "Honestly, Ginger."

"Oh, no." Gin gives her a mock cringe. "Don't break out my full name. I'll stop teasing you right now."

"Ginger?" I give her a playful smile. "I didn't know that was your full name. I guess I figured it was Virginia."

"I took one look at that hair, and I knew," Julia says.

"I would have preferred Ruby or Scarlet," Gin says.

She walks over to her mom and gives her a hug. "Happy birthday. I'm sorry I didn't make you a cake, but I will this weekend. I got your gift a couple months ago. I'll run upstairs and get it."

She looks over at me on her way out of the kitchen and says, "Be right back."

I try not to think about how awkward things could get between her mom and me when we're in here alone. I don't know how I'll respond if she brings up the Sweet Sixteen.

"Dinner smells great," I say. "Anything I can do to help?"

"Thanks. Can you grab that loaf of bread and slice it for me? Across the length of it, so I can make garlic bread?"

She puts down the knife she's using to chop tomatoes and gets a knife off a magnetic holder on the wall, handing it to me. I set it down and wash my hands, drying them on the towel she passes me.

"So, how's senior year going?" she asks.

"Not bad. Busy with it being football season."

"I bet. Where are you going for college?"

I shrug. "Still not sure."

"Well, that's okay. Plenty of time left."

"You think?"

"I do. It's a big decision. Take your time."

"Where did you go?"

Her face lights up with a smile. "Mizzou. I loved it."

Gin comes back into the kitchen holding a small package wrapped up in tissue paper. She sets it on the island, and Julia dries off her hands on a dish towel beside the cutting board before picking it up.

"Thanks, honey. You really didn't have to get me anything."

Gin rolls her eyes. "I always get you something, Mom. Open it."

Julia peels away the layers of white paper, laughing when she sees what's inside. She takes it out and shows it to me.

"My seashell man." She turns to Gin and grins. "We were road-tripping through Maine last summer, and I saw this guy and almost bought him. I was so sorry I didn't."

"I went back for it when you were in another shop," Gin says.

Her mom hugs her again, and I check out the shell man. He's got skinny legs made of broken shells, a round body, and googly eyes glued onto the shell that serves as his head.

"I know it's ugly," Julia says, returning to the tomatoes on the cutting board. "But my mind started spinning with a book idea when I saw him. A story about a man who lives near the ocean and starts to develop the characteristics of fish."

I take the garlic spread she passes to me and put it on the bread with the knife.

"My mom loves your books," I say. "She's read all of them."

Julia smiles and looks genuinely touched. "Oh, how nice. I'll send you with a hardback of my new one that's not out yet."

"She'll go crazy over it. Thanks."

Michael comes in from outside, and Julia shows him her shell man. He admires it, then washes his hands. We all sit down around a round wood table that overlooks a landscaped side yard.

It's not like dinner at my house. No one's eating in a hurry so they can get to the bar and get wasted. No one's quiet because they're afraid of saying anything that might set someone off. We all talk and laugh, and I see what Gin meant about her mom being cool. She's warm and happy. She listens. She keeps adding food to my plate, and to Michael's and Gin's, when they start to get empty.

When Gin talks about what happened at lunch, Julia's eyes fill with tears. She tells Gin she's proud of her for pushing back and defending Raj. As dinner goes on, I start to see where Gin gets her principles from.

Gin insists on clearing the table, and I help her. Since she doesn't have a cake for her mom, she gets a pail of chocolate ice cream from the freezer and puts a scoop in a bowl, then adds a candle to it and lights it. We all sing "Happy Birthday" to Julia, and she blows out the candle. All of us are too full to eat ice cream, but we stay at the table and talk.

The subject of football doesn't come up once. I talk to Gin, Julia, and Michael about everything from politics to my sisters, but no one asks me anything about football.

For the first time in a very long time, I'm just Chase, not Chase the quarterback. It feels good.

After dinner, Gin and I play chess in a sitting room that doesn't look like it gets much use but is still immaculately clean. It's been a while since I've played, but I still beat her in both games we play.

It's after nine when I reluctantly tell Gin I should probably get home. We both have homework to do. Michael said goodbye when he left earlier, and Julia hugs me as we're leaving.

"Come back anytime," she says, passing me a thick book. "And tell your mom she's the first one outside of my publishing house to get this."

"Thanks, she'll be so excited."

"Be back in a bit," Gin says, waving to her mom as we leave.

"Your mom's pretty great," I say as we walk to the car.

"Thanks. I think so, too."

We get in the car, and I realize this was the best evening I've had in a while. I want to ask Gin out, but I don't. After what I've done, I'm lucky she's willing to even be friends.

"Can I ask you a favor?" I say.

"Yeah."

"You know Michelle Zimmerman?"

"Uh-huh. Is she back from rehab?"

"Yeah, she just got back. Will you ask her to sit with you at lunch?"

Gin gives me a skeptical glance. "Me? She doesn't even know me."

"Will you just ask, though?"

She shrugs. "Sure. You want me to ask her if she likes you, too?"

"No." I shake my head for emphasis. "Not at all. It's not like that."

"You'd better not be asking her to join your sex club, Chase. After what she's been through—"

"I'm not. I'm done with that."

"Done with it? As in, not even giving out the roses?" She turns to me, her eyes wide with surprise.

"Long story. But, yeah."

"Wow."

She slows as she approaches my house, then pulls into the driveway.

"You might've mentioned that sooner, you know," she says.

I give her a wry smile. "So you could drill me with questions about it?"

"Something like that," she admits.

"Another night. Guess you'll have to hang out with me again."

"Guess I will."

I open the car door, resisting my urge to lean over and kiss her. "'Night, Gin."

"Goodnight, Chase."

seventeen

Gin

AT LUNCH THE NEXT DAY, Lauren takes the sandwich I pass her and bites into it, eating in silence. She has dark circles under her eyes, and her clothes are wrinkled. I wonder sometimes what motivates her to get up and come to school every morning. It's not her mom, that's for sure. Lauren does more to take care of the household than she does.

"You okay?" I ask her.

She shrugs. "Long night. My little sister threw up at one in the morning. Then again at three, and again at six. I just gave up on sleep at that point."

"That's the worst. Anything I can do to help?"

"No, I'll be okay. I'm gonna crash so hard after work tonight."

I hear my phone buzzing in my bag with a text, and I get it out, assuming it's my mom. But when I look down at the screen, I see a message from Chase.

Chase: Hey Ginger, got a smile for me?

I roll my eyes, unable to keep myself from grinning like an idiot, and look around the cafeteria until I see him standing in the lunch line, his phone in hand. He holds my gaze and smiles back.

"What's going on between you two?" Lauren asks.

I put my phone back in my bag. "Nothing."

"Liar."

Raj sits down next to Lauren, looking back and forth between us and apparently deciding not to say hi just yet.

"Don't be paranoid," I say, twisting open my bottle of water. "Just because I look across the cafeteria, that doesn't mean I'm looking at anyone special."

"You're a fucking liar." Lauren shakes her head. "I'm not an idiot. You got a text from him, you looked over, and then you smiled like a twelve-year-old at a boy band concert."

"Oh, geez. Don't be so melodramatic."

Lauren turns to Raj. "She's got a thing with Chase. The guy who wanted to gangbang her."

Raj stares straight ahead, staying out of it. My aggravation with Lauren rises.

"I do *not* have a thing with him. Stop it," I say in a low tone. "This is how rumors get started."

Lauren curls her lip at me in disgust. "It's one thing to have a crush on his golden-boy looks, but this? What the hell, Gin? Are you gonna be sitting at his lunch table next? Wearing his fucking football jersey with a ribbon in your hair and going to his games?"

"Enough." I silence her with my tone. "Don't take your bad mood and lack of sleep out on me, Lauren."

There's movement next to me, and I look over to see Michelle Zimmerman standing there, biting her lip nervously.

"Hey . . . is this still okay?" she asks me.

I told her this morning that she's welcome to sit with us,

but from the way she silently nodded at me, I didn't think she actually would.

"Of course," I say, gesturing at the open spot next to me. "Guys, you know Michelle, right?"

"Hey, I'm Raj."

Lauren glares at me for a few more seconds before saying, "Yeah, we've partied together before."

"Well . . . thanks for letting me sit here," Michelle says, busying herself with opening her carton of milk and eating her mashed potatoes.

"I actually missed cafeteria food in rehab," she says, laughing lightly. "They only serve super healthy, raw foods there. I lost weight from not eating much."

"Do you feel like rehab helped you?" I ask. "If you don't mind my asking."

"No, you can ask me anything you want. I don't mind talking about it at all. The hardest thing for me is when people just stare at me and say nothing, like I'm some kind of freak." She takes a deep breath. "It helped me a lot. The change of scenery was what I needed. Getting away from the bad habits and situations that had me feeling so . . . hopeless. And my parents came to do therapy with me, and it really set in what my death would've done to them."

"Did you come close to dying?" Lauren asks.

"I don't know . . . my mom found me right away and got me to the hospital."

I just look at her for a few seconds. She looks almost frail, her frame waifish and her eye sockets hollowed. But there's a light in her eyes that doesn't match the rest of her. It's like her eyes are promising there's strength inside her that can't be seen.

"I admire you," I say. "For coming back here and facing this group of judgmental hicks. That had to be hard."

"I think the hardest part was finding out who my real friends were." She shrugs sadly. "Turns out I had none. Once I stopped drinking and getting high, no one I used to hang out with wanted anything to do with me anymore."

"You don't need to be around people like that anyway," I say. "If you're putting all that behind you, I mean."

She nods. "You're right. I just thought they'd . . . care, you know?"

"People are basically self-centered assholes," Lauren says, looking at me. "Using you until something better comes along."

I don't fall into her trap. Lauren's insecurities make her think no one values her, but she comes by it honestly. Neither of her parents has ever valued her as they should.

"Some are," I say, looking at Michelle. "But I'm not. If you ever want to hang out, I'm usually around. When I'm not at play practice or teaching swim lessons."

"Thanks," she says. "I'm so buried in homework right now, but I'm hoping for a social life someday if I ever catch up. They didn't let me keep up with my work in rehab. I just had to focus on therapy and meditation."

"Well, shit." I arch my brows in surprise. "You have a month of makeup work?"

She nods. "Some of my teachers are being really cool and only making me do the big stuff. But Mrs. Luft, not so much."

"Ugh. Calc?"

"No way." She wrinkles her nose. "It's advanced algebra. I'm not a math person."

Raj speaks up. "Well, uh, I am. If you need help, I mean."

"Really?" Michelle smiles at him, and his blush is so deep it's visible even with his dark skin.

"Yeah, anytime." He clears his throat nervously.

My phone buzzes with another text. I glance at Lauren before taking it out to read it.

Chase: You're probably wondering if I took off my shirt for you, but it was cuz I spilled water all over it.

I look over at his table, where's he's wearing not only his T-shirt, but also a huge grin.

Chase: Knew you'd look.

I shake my head, a warm flush creeping up my neck.

"You're disgusting," Lauren says, getting up from the table in a huff.

Michelle gives me a confused look.

"She's just in a mood," Raj says. "She'll be fine tomorrow."

I'm not so sure, though. Lauren's never been one to forgive easily. And I can see why she's upset with me. Chase is the captain of the football team—the leader of everything that disgusts us.

I see him changing, though. And I'm not turning my back on him. I hope my longtime crush on him isn't clouding my vision. I believe Chase when he says he's done with the Sweet Sixteen. That's not for me to share with anyone, though. I just hope Lauren will get a chance to see for herself that things aren't exactly as they seem.

Even when she's grouchy and brutally honest, she's my best friend. I don't have enough friends to be trading a new one for an old one.

eighteen

Chase

I'M TRYING TO KEEP MY head down, staying focused on my classes and football. I can't help getting distracted by Gin too. She invites me home for dinner again, which serves two purposes—I get to spend more time with her, and I manage to avoid my dad, who will jump my ass about committing to a school.

By Thursday, I've only been at home to sleep, but I find out my system isn't gonna save me forever when I see a note from my dad on the kitchen counter in the morning, next to the book from Gin's mom that my mom's nearly done with already.

You need to commit to Bama. Be home for dinner tonight.

Fuck. I crumple the paper and toss it in the trash, grabbing the toast my mom hands me on my way out the door.

"See you tonight?" she asks hopefully.

I hear the plea in her question—*save me from feeling your father's wrath if you're not here.*

"Yeah. I'll come home after practice. I'm not ready to commit to a school yet, though."

She sighs softly. "I just don't want you to miss out, Chase. That's where your dad's coming from too, even though it doesn't feel that way."

"It feels like he wants to make the decisions and have me live with them. But it's my decision, Mom."

She nods, but her expression is skeptical. Like me, she's always let Dad bully her into whatever he wants. I'm not letting him have his way this time, though.

Sam honks his horn from the driveway.

"I've gotta go, Mom. See you tonight."

She smiles and waves me out the door. When I get into Sam's passenger seat, he greets me with, "Hey, man. Got a favor to ask."

"Yeah, what?"

"Can we pick Felicity White this week? It's the only way I'm ever getting between her legs."

I shake my head, disgust flooding through me. "Won't be up to me, man. I'm done with all that."

He laughs as he backs out of the driveway. "Whatever, asshole. Just do this for me, okay?"

"I'm serious. I'm done. No more choosing girls, no more roses, no more parties."

Sam pulls up to the stop sign and steps on the brake, turning to me. "What the fuck are you talking about, Matthews?"

"I'm. Done."

"But . . . how do you get to make a decision like that? That's bullshit."

"The rest of you can do what you want, but I'm out." I point at the car on the other side of the intersection. "It's your turn to go."

"Why?" He turns to face the road and drives, his expression stunned.

"I don't feel right about it."

He scoffs. "Because of Gin Fielding?"

"Because of me. I mean, did you hear what you just said? Felicity wouldn't sleep with you unless she was part of the Sweet Sixteen? You know how fucked up that is?"

His silence tells me he doesn't.

"This just seems random," he says. "Why all of a sudden? It's senior year. How do you think the team's gonna feel about this?"

"Like I said, the rest of you can do what you want. No one better get pissed at me over what I choose to do or not do."

"So, what then? You want me to just tell them you're not doing it?"

"You can, or I will."

He shakes his head, his expression still etched with disbelief. "But . . . what about meeting after practice to choose someone today?"

"I won't be there."

"You'll change your mind, though. I'm not saying anything to anyone."

I won't change my mind, but there's no reason to argue with him about it. We ride in silence the rest of the way to school. When we get there, I walk in on my own, leaving Sam trailing behind.

Something tells me I'd better ask Gin for a ride to school tomorrow.

BY LUNCH, EVERYONE KNOWS. I didn't think Sam would stay quiet, and I was right. Guys are coming up to me asking me what's going on, all of them looking dazed when I tell them I'm done with the Sweet Sixteen.

"It's Gin, isn't it?" Jack Pearson says bitterly. "You fucked her, and now she doesn't want you fucking anyone else. I see the way you look at her."

I shove him into a row of lockers, anger flowing hot and fast through my veins. "Say one more thing about her, and I'll break your fucking hand," I say, pointing a finger in his face.

His eyes narrow. "You're gonna break your best wide receiver's hand? Fuck no."

"Say something about her and find out," I challenge.

He keeps his eyes locked on mine in a few seconds of silent contemplation.

"I'm gonna be late for class," he finally says, shoving off the locker and leaving.

I don't want to deal with the bullshit in the cafeteria, so I take my lunch tray to Coach's office and eat there, talking about this week's game with him. It's almost time to leave for class when my phone buzzes with a text.

Gin: Wow. Are you trying to be more hated than me? Because it's working.

Me: They'll get over it.

Gin: I hope so. Jack Pearson is looking at me like he wants to kill me with his bare hands.

Me: He won't lay a hand on you.

Gin: Are you sure this is what you want?

Me: It's not even like that anymore. This is what I have to do.

Gin: Be careful, okay?

Me: Don't worry about me. See you at play practice.

Gin: Need a ride to school tomorrow?

Me: Yeah, thanks.

I put my phone in my bag and get up to go to class, but Coach Carter stops me.

"Sit back down, Chase. I'll write you an excuse for being late."

I reseat myself in the chair across from his desk, looking at him.

"What's up, Coach?"

"Your dad came to see me the other day. He's concerned about you not committing to a school yet, and frankly, I am too. Can we talk this through and figure it out?"

I lean forward, resting my elbows on my knees. My dad's not letting up on this.

"He wants me to go to Bama."

"And what do you want?"

I shake my head. "I'm not sure yet. I like Penn State a lot, though."

"They're both great programs. I think you'd do well at either."

"Thanks."

"But the coaches aren't gonna wait forever, Chase. It's already way past time."

I nod but say nothing.

"I think your dad would be happier with you committing to Penn State than not committing anywhere at this point. Can you bring that up with him?"

"I can, but . . ."

I can't tell him what comes after the but.

. . . but I'm not sure if he'll punch my mom in a fit of anger over not getting his way.

. . . but I don't know if my mom and sisters will be safe if I'm that far away.

. . . but I'm concerned that my decision is being influenced by a certain girl who's going to NYU next year, whom I want to be as close to as possible.

"You've played for me for four years, Chase. I know you.

Level with me."

"My dad's controlling," I say, choosing my words carefully.

Coach smiles at that. "Yeah. Even more so on this because it's one of the last things he *can* control in terms of your football."

I hadn't thought of it that way, but he's right.

"Do I choose for myself only, or do I . . . keep my family in mind?" I ask.

"You need to choose the coach and program that gets you the most excited. That's very important. You're gonna get drafted, Chase, and the decisions you make from here on out are crucial."

I exhale heavily and stare at the swirling, faded gray pattern on the linoleum floor. "I'm usually okay under pressure," I say softly.

Coach laughs at that. "Son, you're *great* under pressure. But there are different kinds of pressure. My advice is to choose one and move forward. You've worked too hard to make a misstep now."

I nod. "Thanks, Coach. I will." I meet his eyes across the desk. "Can I ask you another question?"

"Of course."

"Do you know about the Sweet Sixteen?"

He furrows his brow. "The first round of the NCAA tournament?"

"No, I mean . . ." I clear my throat and try again. "The parties at Skylar Adair's place after games—do you know what goes on there?"

His lips thin into a serious expression. "I think it's best I know as little as possible about that."

He takes out a yellow notepad and starts scrawling me a note for class.

"Why is that?" I ask.

He looks up from the note. "What?"

"Why do you think it's best that you know as little as possible about the parties?"

We stare at each other for a few seconds as he tries to come up with an answer.

"Why are you asking me this, Chase? You know why."

"Yeah, I do. Because it's wrong. And you know it's wrong and don't want to be responsible for not doing anything about it. So you just look the other way."

He gives me a stern look. "Where's this coming from? If I policed my players and cracked down on everything they did that's against the rules, I wouldn't have any damn players left."

"You tell us to be gentlemen. We all go and rake yards for senior citizens and paint concession stands to give back, but . . . there is no giving back what we've taken."

"I'm not sure what you mean, Chase. I know there's some drinking at those parties, but as long as no one's driving after . . ."

"Not the drinking."

He sighs heavily. "Just tell me what's on your mind."

I sit back, folding my hands in my lap. "I've decided I'm no longer going to be a part of a certain unnamed activity that happens at those parties, and most of the guys are pissed at me over it. I'm not backing down, though."

He nods slightly. "Whatever it is, it's your decision."

"There's gonna be blowback. Probably a call for a new team captain."

"Won't happen. You're my captain, and you're staying my captain. You've got a level head on your shoulders, and I trust that you're following your gut on this."

I stand up. "Thanks. And you may not want to hear this, but . . . there are guys on the team with shitty parents. If no one at home's telling them how to be a gentleman, they need you to.

And you need to do a better job with it."

He narrows his eyes. "In what regard?"

"How to treat women. Girls, whatever."

He grimaces, then nods.

"I'm one of the guys with a shitty example at home, but I still know right from wrong." I shake my head sadly. "Took me a long time to get here, though. And if you don't stand up and face what's going on, you're not the man I thought you were."

"I understand." His expression is solemn as he passes me the note. "See you at practice."

I walk to class, and when I get there, my usual seat between Sam and Clay has been moved over to the side of the room, where it sits alone.

Fucking babies. I stride over to it and sit down, showing no reaction.

And I feel a fresh stab of guilt over what I did to Gin. Thanks to that rose, this is what her life's been like lately too.

Sam and Clay are supposed to be more than friends to me. We're supposed to be brothers. Seems I overestimated them by a lot. I can't find it in me to even give a shit, though.

nineteen

Gin

FRIDAY IS A TOTAL SHITSHOW at school.

When I walk into the building after a nearly silent car ride with Chase and pull on the handle of my locker, I feel something thick and wet on my fingers. My stomach turns so hard and fast I fear I may puke right there on the floor. Instead, I race to the bathroom, my hand out in front of me like it's carrying a plague, and when I make it, I crank up the hot water and coat my entire hand in gooey soap, rinsing it in the water before washing my hands together three more times.

I don't even want to think about what it was. *Is*, actually. I still need to get into my locker. Fortunately, I was an office runner my freshman year, fetching coffee and doing errands for the administrative staff, so I go see the ladies there. They give me sanitizer, call the custodian, and ask him to remove the handle of my locker for me, and give me an excuse to be late for class.

When I get to third period, I'm horrified to see that someone painted "Gin is a cunt" on the teacher's chalkboard. Fucking white *paint*. When the teacher walks in and sees it, her face pales and she immediately moves class to the library for the day.

I want to skip lunch, but I'm not giving anyone the satisfaction. When I sit down at the table, I give Lauren a glare that just *dares* her to fuck with me today.

"I'm sorry," she says softly, quickly adding, "About the chalkboard, I mean."

A half smile pulls at my lips. "Uh-huh. Cause there's nothing *else* you should be sorry for?"

She rolls her eyes dramatically. "All right, I'm sorry I was an asshole, okay? It's just hard to watch all this. That fucker doesn't deserve you."

"I'm okay. I promise."

"All this shit that's happening to you is because of him, though."

I glance around the cafeteria, looking for Chase. "I'm pretty sure he's not having the best day either."

Lauren grunts skeptically. "I didn't hear about anyone writing '*Chase is a cocksucking motherfucker*' on a chalkboard today."

"Yeah, because *too many syllables*." I meet her gaze across the table. "Roper kids, remember? They can't spell those words."

She breaks into a grin. Raj and Michelle sit down together on the other side of our table, him explaining something mathematic to her.

I pass Lauren a sandwich, leaving mine in the bag. Craning my neck, I look around the cafeteria for Chase.

Where is he? From what little I've overheard, he's tied with me for first place on most everyone's shit list.

Apparently, the football team still gathered and waited this morning, thinking Chase would be there to give out a rose. When he didn't show, Sam Stockwell offered to take over and do it, but most of the guys didn't want to go along with that.

So for the first time since I've been at Roper High School, no one got a rose on a Friday morning before a football game. I can't imagine Chase will just come take his seat at his usual table like nothing's amiss.

Girls are stunned and upset over Chase's change of heart, and the football players I've seen today either look despondent or furious. I find the whole thing ridiculous and sad.

Chase didn't say where he was going when we got to school this morning, and I didn't ask. He seemed sullen and withdrawn. I can't help wondering if it's because he was second-guessing his decision to give up the Sweet Sixteen.

He never shows up for lunch, and for whatever reason, it really pisses me off. I've shown up in the cafeteria every day for the past two weeks, and it hasn't been easy. But I'm not running away from the decision I made. I'm not afraid of the consequences.

I use several tissues to open my locker in the afternoon, after the custodian sanitized and replaced my locker handle. Then I go from class to class, my anger building as the day goes on.

At the end of the day, I'm bent over loading books into my locker, passing people calling me everything from lesbian to bitch. To my back, of course. I don't think they'd be brave enough to say it to my face. Cowards.

I keep my expression neutral, relieved there's no play practice today and I can just go home and not venture out until Monday. As I stand up and turn around, though, something flies into my face. I gasp and step back, reaching for my eye to feel what it is.

Spit.

I caught a flash of Jack Pearson's evil grin before I closed both eyes, and now I'm furious enough to take him on. Fuck him. Fuck all of them. They're a bunch of emotionally stunted assholes, and I'm done taking their shit.

I dig through my bag and find some tissues, wiping off my face. Several girls are giggling nearby as they watch me, and I feel tears threatening to spill from my eyes.

Not because I'm about to crumble, but because I'm just that angry. I'm mad enough to punch someone. For two weeks, I've endured nonstop bullshit because I don't want to be gangbanged.

I've had it.

Slinging my bag over my shoulder, I move down the hallway so fast my hair flies out behind me. I'm on a mission, and it's an emotionally charged one. If I can't find Chase in these hallways, I'll go confront him at practice. I'd walk onto the field in the middle of a game if I had to. My tolerance had a good run, but it went up in a mushroom cloud of ruin when Jack spat in my face.

Chase is at his locker, his tall, wide-shouldered frame dwarfing the open metal door. I stop when I get there, arms crossed in front of me.

"Hey," he says. "What's—"

"We need to talk."

"Everything okay?"

"No." I overenunciate the word, my face hot with anger.

"Did I do something?" He gives me a confused look.

I shake my head. "You've got about one minute to get me someplace with fewer people, or I'll blow my top right here."

"Uh . . ." He looks up and down the hallway, which is still full of students. "Your car?"

"Fine."

I turn on a heel and lead the way, my fury building steam with every step. Chase follows me out the main entrance and down the stone steps, people staring curiously at us the whole way.

Staring, but not saying a word. Because they don't dare call me a bitch, cunt, or lesbian with him five feet behind me. And for some reason, that incites my anger even further.

We've almost made it to the parking lot, but I can't walk another step without saying something. I turn and glare at him.

"Where were you at lunch today?"

He arches his brows in surprise. "I had lunch in my coach's office."

"Why?"

He scoffs and looks at me like I'm clueless. "To avoid the blowback."

"Yeah?" I narrow my eyes and cross my arms. "What kind of blowback did you get today?"

"Gin, I have no idea why you're pissed at me. Don't play games about it, just tell me."

I ask in a louder tone. "What kind of blowback, Chase?"

He sighs heavily. "The guys are all pissed at me, obviously. No one wants to sit by me in class or even talk to me."

"*And*?" I demand.

"And *what*, Gin?" He raises his voice to match mine.

"There better be more than that."

He scoffs again. "Yeah? I'm not getting what you think I deserve, is that it?"

I take a step closer to him, leaving just a foot between us. "There was bodily fluid on my locker handle this morning. Someone painted 'Gin is a cunt' on a chalkboard, and my entire class had to be moved. Jack spit in my fucking *eye*, Chase."

His expression darkens. "Jack Pearson?"

I throw my arms in the air. "Yeah, Jack Pearson! I've been called every name in the book today. So many times. I've been stared at and whispered about, all because *you* didn't give out that stupid rose this morning."

I poke a finger into his chest, but he doesn't seem to notice. "Isn't this what you wanted? All that talk about it being disgusting and wrong, and now you're pissed off that I'm not doing it anymore?"

I ball my hands into fists at my sides. "No, I'm not pissed that you're not doing it anymore, you asshole. I'm pissed that *I* have to feel the fallout. All of it. While you sit in your coach's office and avoid reality."

He looks up at the sky, putting a hand on the back of his neck. "Come on, Gin. I'm doing my best here. I'm out, for good. But having football players brawling in the cafeteria isn't good for anyone."

"And Jack spitting on me—who is *that* good for?"

Chase's eyes bulge in a look of frustration. "That's not my fucking fault, Gin! I'll handle it now that I know, and if I'd been there to defend you, I would've."

"I don't want you defending me!" I shove his chest with my palms, but he doesn't move. "I show up, Chase. To this miserable school every day. To the cafeteria at lunchtime. I took a stand, and I'm not ashamed of it. But *you*? You took a stand and then ducked and ran."

He shakes his head. "Not fucking fair, Gin. Because I had lunch in my coach's office?"

"Not just because of that. When Michelle needed a friend, did you step up and be a friend to her, in front of everyone? No, you secretly asked me to do it."

There's a spark of anger in his darkened blue eyes. He leans in and speaks in a low tone. "You think it's a coincidence, Gin? What happened to her, and me feeling guilt so strong I can't even breathe sometimes? If I even *look* at her, I feel sick. Do you see what she's become? And it started with something *I* did. She's the walking proof of what a miserable prick I am. And that's why I asked you—because you're strong and . . . good."

I close my eyes for a couple seconds, resisting my urge to back down. These things need to be said.

"Chase, you decided to take a stand, and that's a good thing. So, do it. Stand tall and be proud."

He looks away in disgust. "I've got nothing to be proud of. I decided to stop using girls, sure, but how many have I already used? How many have I damaged?"

I keep my eyes locked on his. "Own it, then. Apologize. Move forward."

"How do you apologize for that, Gin? What words are good enough?"

"Sincere ones. If you're sorry, don't hang your head and hide."

He scrubs a hand down his face. "Look, I hear you. But I can't . . . I have to stay on the team. Football is my ticket out of here."

"Right," I say bitterly. "So you're just gonna keep playing, not be *part* of the gangbanging, but not condemn anyone else doing it, either?"

"I said I think it's wrong. What more do you want from me?"

I shake my head sadly. "Nothing. And I mean that in every way, Chase. I want nothing more from you. Don't text, don't come to play practice, don't ask me for rides. Just stay away from me."

I turn around and walk to my car, shaking all over. It's not until I've gotten in my car, buckled up, and pulled out onto the road that I let the tears fall.

Finally. After two weeks, I cry.

I never would've thought a single rose would ruin me this way.

twenty

Chase

THE KNOCK ON MY CLOSED bedroom door makes me close my eyes and exhale deeply. My dad must want to go another round over committing to a school. The more I refuse to do it, the closer he seems to get to realizing that he can't force me to do what he wants.

It's not like when I was playing Pee Wee football, looking to him on the sidelines for signals instead of my coach. I'm not falling into line this time.

I don't respond, hoping he might go away, and a couple seconds later, the door is slowly pushed open a few inches.

"Chase?" my sister Alyssa calls into the room.

I'm lying down on the bed, and I sit up when I see her.

"Hey, you can come in."

She opens the door, slides into the room, and closes it behind her.

"Can I be in here for a little while?" she whispers.

"Yeah." I pat the spot beside me on the bed, and she comes over and sits down. "What's going on?"

"Mom's crying." She looks at the ground, sounding ashamed to be admitting it.

In our house, we rarely talk about the elephant in the room, which is my dad's drinking and anger. The rest of us seem to think that not acknowledging it somehow makes it less real.

"Do you know why?" I ask Alyssa.

"Dad's yelling at her. He seems mad about everything. He told Cassie she looks like a whore in the shirt she's wearing."

I didn't hear any of that over the music I have on. I shake my head and put my arm around Alyssa.

"You stay in here as long as you want, okay?"

She nods. "He won't mess with you because tomorrow's game day."

Her words are like a punch in my gut. She's right. Dad doesn't start shit with me on Thursdays or Fridays. This is the night before game day, and he wants me getting my head into the right space for tomorrow night.

I can't possibly think about football, though. Gin and I haven't spoken in almost a week, and it's making me crazy. I didn't realize how much I'd started to rely on her until she wasn't there anymore.

If I pass her in the hallway, she's always looking somewhere else, deliberately avoiding eye contact. I stopped going to play practice because I know she doesn't want me there. At first, I thought things would blow over, but now I don't think so.

Gin's strong. She's not one to cave easily. And even though I think she overreacted, I get where she's coming from. She doesn't seem to understand the pressure I'm under, though.

A few of my teammates are with me. Ben Hart, a junior, was

the first to have the balls to approach me and tell me he agrees with my decision. A few other guys followed, but none of the heavy hitters who are on the field with me at kickoff every Friday night.

Those lights that shine on us weekly every fall made us feel like rock stars. Invincible town heroes. Entitled assholes who treated girls like trash.

I look over at my little sister and swallow hard, a fresh wave of shame hitting me.

"Hey. Don't you ever, ever let a guy disrespect you, you hear me? The way Dad treats Mom—don't you ever put up with that. Your body is . . . it's *yours*, and you shouldn't let anyone treat your body like it's there for their stress relief or entertainment."

She nods, her eyes wide and solemn.

"I've made mistakes," I admit.

"You have?"

"Yeah. But I've learned from them, and I hope I can help you avoid making the same kinds of mistakes."

Alyssa turns to the side so she's facing me. "Kids at school are saying stuff about you. I tell them to shut their faces."

I pat her knee and smile. "Thanks, kid. I'll be okay."

"You *are* going to college, right?"

"Of course I am. Why are you asking me that?"

She shrugs. "I heard Dad telling Mom he thinks you don't want to go."

"Ah."

That explains his rage. The old man thinks I'm gonna end up like him—his chance for redemption shot down. Makes me want to wait even longer to commit to a school.

"Can I tell you a secret?" I turn and look down at Alyssa.

Her eyes shine happily. "Yes. I won't tell anyone."

"When it's time for you to start college, you'll be able to go anywhere you want. I'll be in the NFL by then, unless I get injured in college, which I'm gonna do my best to avoid. I'm gonna take care of you then. You'll have a car and nice clothes and all your classes paid for."

"Really?" She grins hopefully.

"Yep. So for the next four years, once you start high school, here's what I want you to do: work hard in all your classes. Get the best grades you can. Don't get too distracted by boys. Make good decisions, and if you need help knowing which decisions to make, you can ask me. Can you do all that for me?"

"Yes."

"I'm gonna do the same for Cass, but she doesn't know that yet. I'll still be in college when she starts college, so she'll have to take out loans, but I can pay them back after I get drafted."

"I'm so excited," she says, wrapping her arms around herself.

"Me too. And can I tell you one more secret?"

She nods enthusiastically.

"Everyone thinks the guys I play football with are my team. And they kinda are. But the truth is, you and Cassie and Mom are my team. The four of us, we're gonna be okay. I'm gonna make sure of it."

"Not Dad?"

I shake my head. "He's not on our team."

The song on my stereo ends, and the sound of my Dad raging about something takes its place. Alyssa sighs softly and looks at the ground.

"I'm going out there," I say to her. "Find a book in here to read or something, okay?"

She nods, her eyes wide with worry. "Cassie's not a whore."

"No. Remember this, okay? Dad's anger has nothing to do with anyone but himself."

"Okay."

I get up and head for the door, giving her a reassuring smile over my shoulder on the way out. As soon as I'm in the hallway, I hear Dad yelling from the kitchen.

"We just had meatloaf last week! I'm so fucking sick of meatloaf."

"I thought you liked it," I hear my mom say. "I'm sorry."

I shake my head and clench my fists as I walk into the kitchen.

"What do you want?" my dad demands. "If you're not here to tell me you're ready to commit to Bama, turn around and walk back to your room."

I walk over to the kitchen counter, which Mom is leaning her back against, and stand next to her.

"You want to bitch about dinner now?" I ask my dad in a level tone.

"Excuse me?" His expression twists with shock.

I don't know what's come over me, or why. Maybe it's all the stress that's been squeezing me like a vise, but I feel changed. I'm not leaving this room.

"Come on," I say. "You're tough enough to say it when she's in here alone, be tough enough to say it when someone bigger than you is standing here."

"This is none of your goddamned business." He points a finger at me. "Get out of here. Go watch your film or wring your hands about what school to pick before you've got none left to pick from."

"No, *you* get out of here," I say, feeling more confident with every word. "Take your sorry ass to the bar—"

"Chase," my mom says softly.

"—and leave the rest of us to eat our delicious meatloaf in peace."

"Listen here." My dad advances on us, and I feel my mom

flinch. "This is *my* house, and—"

"Get out right now, or I'm not playing tomorrow night." I fold my arms over my chest. "I'll tell Coach I need a mental health day to recover from my dad pushing my mom around."

"Chase!" My mom looks up at me, shocked.

"I swear to you, I'll do it," I tell my dad.

He narrows his eyes at me in disgust, swipes his keys from the counter, and leaves.

"What are you doing?" my mom asks me.

"Standing up," I say, remembering Gin's words. "You deserve better than him, Mom."

"Honey, he means well."

I roll my eyes as the engine of my dad's truck roars to life and he backs out of the driveway.

"Don't waste your breath defending him to me, Mom," I say, heading back out of the room.

I feel a twinge of satisfaction as I walk back to my room, thinking about his expression when he knew he was beat.

Nothing means more to my dad than his progeny leading Roper High to glory in every game.

There's still a war, and I won't have a way to win it for a long time. But today, I won a battle, and given the shitty week I've had, I'll take the small victory.

twenty-one

Gin

MADISON MISSES HER CUE FOR the second time in a row, and I have to keep myself from snapping in frustration. It's not my job to feed her lines or remind her of cues. I let Mr. Douglas handle it, and I slip in my earbuds.

It's Monday, and it's been eleven days since Chase and I argued. At this point, I don't just want to count the days, but also the hours. I miss him.

He seems to be under just as much heat as I am. Last week, word flew around the school fast that Chase had punched Jack Pearson, giving him a nasty black eye. I knew he'd done it as retribution for Jack spitting on me, and my heart had swelled with affection.

How sick is that, me going weak-kneed over a guy punching someone for me? But since that guy is Chase, and it was Jack he punched, I couldn't help it.

A line has been drawn on the football team. Chase leads the

small group of opponents against the Sweet Sixteen. Jack leads the group of swaggering knuckle-draggers who are angry over being cheated out of their fun.

I'm proud of Chase, and I want to tell him that. But I ache for him to call or text or find me at play practice, and tell me he misses me and he's sorry. I need to hear him say that I matter to him, and not in response to me chasing after him like a lost puppy dog.

I paint in silence, lost in my music and my feelings, until Mr. Douglas approaches me. I pull out my earbuds and stand to see what he wants.

"How's our set coming, my esteemed art director?" he asks.

"Pretty good. We're back on schedule."

"What did you make for Ellie's bedroom?"

"Just a wall with a bed and posters painted on it."

He gives me a thumbs-up. "Still need an MIT banner?"

"If possible, that would be great. I left a space for it on Ellie's wall."

"Mrs. Morganstern brought one in for us. I left it on top of my filing cabinet." He takes a key ring from his pocket and passes it to me. "The one with the Cardinals logo opens my classroom door if you want to go get it."

I take the keys. "Sure, I'll go now." I arch my brows at him. "Or—I'll steal your car and head for the border."

"Ha! You want to take that hunk of junk off my hands, be my guest."

I smile and put my earbud back in, Adele's voice filling my ears. Mr. Douglas's classroom is about the same distance from me no matter what route I take, but I decide to cut through the gym, just in case Chase is lingering outside the locker room.

I'm pathetic and I know it. The football team is always changed and on the field by now, but I'll take even a small chance of running into Chase.

Maybe it would give us a chance to talk without one of us having to apologize. Or maybe I'll just swallow my stupid pride and admit I overreacted.

I have absolutely no experience with boys, but when I talked to my mom about Chase this weekend, she told me just to do what feels right.

After eleven days of radio silence, talking to Chase again is what feels right. I miss our secret looks as we pass in the hallway and his playful nightly texts.

The gym is empty today—the cheerleaders must be practicing outside. I walk through it, slowing by the boys' locker room door just in case Chase comes out.

Nothing, though. I'm past the door and about to exit the gym in disappointment when an arm hooks around me from behind. I freeze, shocked, and a hand presses something over my mouth.

Duct tape, I think. I'm picked up and thrown over someone's shoulder, my heart pounding frantically. I kick, which is all I can do since my arms are being held tight to my sides. As I twist my body, trying to get free, I see who has me, and my heart feels like it may stop.

Jack Pearson.

He struggles to get the locker room door open, using his foot so he can keep both arms holding me captive.

The harder I struggle against him, the harder it gets to breathe through my nose, which is my only option now. I'm getting light-headed, so I try to focus just on a few deep breaths.

Jack sets me on the ground in front of some lockers, caging me in with his forearms pressed to the lockers on either side of me. The swelling on his eye has gone down since last week, but it's still a mean shade of purple.

"Chase isn't here to protect you this time, is he?" He pushes his sweaty face just a couple inches from mine. "You ruined everything, you bitch. We lost our captain, I lost my friend. All because you think you're too good to spread your fucking legs."

My chest heaves in and out as I breathe, the difficulty almost as terrifying as whatever Jack's about to do.

"You're gonna make this right." His tone is low, his lips so close to my face I turn to the side, trying to avoid him.

I don't have breath to spare, but a muffled scream comes out as a hum in my chest as Jack grabs the waistband of my gray sweats and pulls them down.

Horror overwhelms me as the air hits my bare thighs. I'm still light-headed, and now I'm about to vomit too. If I do, and Jack leaves the tape on my mouth, I could choke.

Stay calm, Gin.

I think of my mom and what she'd tell me right now. *Stay calm. Think. Don't give in to the fear.*

Jack's working on getting his own pants down now, and I use the opportunity to shove him away from me. He doesn't go very far, though. He's so much bigger and stronger that he has his hands wrapped around my upper arms in a matter of seconds, and he slams me against the lockers, pain shooting through the back of my head as it strikes the metal.

"Fight if you want," he sneers and winks. "I'll just enjoy it more."

I head-butt him, desperate to fight back, but I don't hit him hard enough to hurt much. He wraps a hand around my hair and shoves my head down on the locker room's wood bench, my cheek burning from the impact.

"It would have been easier at the cabin," he says, shoving his pants down with his free hand.

Suddenly, I see a part of Jack Pearson I never *wanted* to see. I realize how close I am to being raped, and I stop thinking and just react. I grab at him with both hands, clawing and pinching.

He slams my head against the bench again, sending stars into my field of vision. I don't let up, though. I grab his pathetic little dick and scratch with all my strength. I pull on his nuts and squeeze his balls so hard he cries out in pain.

"Fucking bitch!" He instinctively covers his parts with both hands, and I stand up, ripping the tape from my mouth.

I gulp in air as Jack lunges for me, and I kick and push at him to keep him from getting both arms around me. My terror seems to be giving me extra strength. Every time he gets closer, I back away and somehow manage to keep him from pinning me again.

"You. Owe. Me." He gives me a murderous glare and then lunges, taking hold of both my wrists. I drive a knee up into his balls, twisting so hard and fast I feel a sharp pull in my back.

He folds over in pain, both hands on his crotch as he howls, and I make a run for it. Adrenaline pumps through me hard and fast, a voice inside telling me this may be the only chance I get to escape.

I move as fast as I can, holding my pants up just enough to get a hand on the door handle and open it. When I'm in the gym, I break into a run, pulling my pants all the way up as I go.

I can breathe again. I'm free. But I'm not safe yet. I have to get to people.

Going back in the direction I came, I decide Mr. Douglas is my best hope. I know he's in the theater right now. I get to the other gym door, open it, and burst wild-eyed into the hallway.

Empty, except for Chase.

"Gin!" He drops his helmet in front of the water fountain he was drinking from and runs toward me. "Oh my God, are you okay?"

He reaches for me, but he stops his hands in midair. "I don't want to hurt you."

Tears flood my eyes as I look at him. *Now,* I'm safe. I just want him to hold on to me right now, whether it hurts or not.

"I—" I'm interrupted by the opening of the door I just walked out of.

Jack's expression is dark, and his hair and clothes are a mess. He looks from me to Chase, then abruptly turns back and closes the door.

Chase cups my cheek gently. "Tell me you're okay."

I nod, tears clouding my vision.

"I have to go get him, Gin. Before he has a chance to . . . shower." He cringes, his own eyes glassy with tears. "Go find Mr. Douglas. Call the police. Do that for me, okay?"

"Yes," I whisper.

He presses a tender kiss to my forehead, then runs through the door after Jack. I make it the last hundred yards back to the theater, not seeing or hearing anything around me until I find Mr. Douglas.

"Gin." He looks at me, his brow furrowed in concern. "What happened?"

I swallow hard and find my voice. "Call the police."

twenty-two

Chase

GIN SETS A PILLOW ON my lap and then gingerly lowers her head onto it, curling up and closing her eyes.

"I've still got a headache," she murmurs. "Even with all the medicine they gave me at the hospital."

"Just relax," I say, carefully brushing the hair away from her face.

One side of her face is swollen and purple with bruises. Every time I look at her, my stomach turns in disgust. I'm not just angry at Jack this time. Giving him a black eye isn't going to help.

I want to kill him. I feel an even deeper rage toward him than I do my father. Jack didn't just beat Gin. He tried to rape her. If she hadn't somehow fought him off, she would have been sexually assaulted in the locker room I'd been standing in just a few minutes before.

It's been a hell of an evening. Gin's mom took her to the hospital, and the tests, treatments, and police interviews took a couple hours. I sat in the waiting room with Lauren, Raj, and Michelle, where Lauren gave me a death stare the entire time. Our principal, Mr. Schilling, and our assistant principal, Mrs. Metz, stayed outside Gin's room the whole time to be there for her and her mom.

Things are going to change now. I got that from the look on Mrs. Metz's face when she asked me to go to a conference room for a few minutes as we waited for Gin to be released. Mrs. Metz's eyes swam with judgment and determination as she asked me about the Sweet Sixteen.

I told her everything. As far as I'm concerned, all bets are off. There's no such thing as brotherhood or loyalty between Jack and me anymore, or any of the other guys who've been part of those parties.

I'll own the consequences for what I've done. In a way, it's a relief. I've been condemning myself over it, but I know I can't even begin to move on until I feel the full weight of what's sure to come.

Maybe I'll get kicked off the team. Hell, our entire football program could be suspended. But so be it. I can't think long-term right now. Who gives a shit about protecting my college prospects after what happened today?

My phone blew up with texts all evening; some messages were people mining for information, but others were people saying Jack had taken things too far.

"How are you feeling?" I ask Gin.

"I'm okay," she says softly.

She's been the one comforting her mom and me, instead of the other way around. I knew Gin was strong, but tonight, I'm finding I didn't know just *how* strong.

When Mr. Schilling told her she's excused from school for

the rest of the week to heal, and the next week if needed, she shook her head.

"I'll take tomorrow off," she said. "That'll be enough."

Mr. Schilling cleared his throat and tried again. "I think at least the whole week, though, don't you?" He looked at Gin's mom. "Seeing you like this could be disturbing for other students."

"It *should* disturb them," Gin said. "Sexual assault isn't just words on a pamphlet, you know."

"I couldn't agree more," her mom said. "But you *weren't* raped, right? Not at all? Because if you were—"

"No. I clawed the shit out of his dick and balls, so they should be out of commission for a while."

Mr. Schilling looked horrified; Mrs. Metz couldn't hold back a smile. I'd never been prouder of another person in my life.

Jack is a lot bigger than Gin, and he's a hell of a lot stronger. But somehow, she found a way.

When I caught Jack earlier, I got in some good hits. He got me back once in the jaw, but I broke his fucking nose.

"I never imagined I'd be here," Gin says from my lap, her words slightly slurred from the medications she's on.

"I'm gonna break Jack's nose again after it heals," I mutter.

"No, I don't mean that . . . I'm *fine*, Chase, really. Relieved. And tired. I mean . . . I never thought you'd be here . . . on my couch, with my head on your lap."

I smile down at her. "Yeah, me either."

"Do you know?" she murmurs, looking at me expectantly.

"Do I know what, Ginger?"

"That I've had a crush on you forever. Since before junior high?"

She wouldn't tell me this if she weren't so loopy from the hospital drugs. But there's something about seeing her this way, so vulnerable, that makes me feel like now it's *me* who has a crush on *her*.

"I know now," I say, lightly running my fingers over her hair. "And it's a mutual crush, just so you know."

"But not before," she says so softly I almost can't hear her. "Before . . . you didn't even know I existed."

"I was an asshole," I admit. "But I see you now, Gin. Trust me. I see you even when I'm not looking at you."

A smile curls up the corners of her lips as she closes her eyes.

"I'll tell you a secret in return," I say.

I'm pretty sure she's nearly asleep, so I keep stroking her hair, thinking about the way to say this. But it's one of those things there's no easy way to describe.

"My dad beats my mom," I finally say. "I've never told anyone that. It's the dirty secret in our house. He hits her when he's drunk, when he's pissed off . . . when it's Tuesday. He doesn't need a fucking reason. And when I saw what Jack did to you, I thought about my mom. About how I wish she was as strong as you, to go to the police."

Gin's still and silent, so I don't think she heard me. But then she shifts a little, finding my hand and weaving her fingers into mine.

And we stay like that as she falls asleep. I drift off myself, and when I wake up close to midnight, I carefully slide out from beneath her head, cover her up, and brush a soft kiss over her lips before letting myself out a side door, locking it behind me.

I NEVER THOUGHT I'D BE disgusted to be seen in a Roper football jersey, but today, I am. It's Friday—game day.

I tried to quit the team yesterday when I dumped my jerseys on Coach Carter's desk at lunch. He told me he didn't accept and would send a freshman over to my house to return them that night. That meant nothing to me and I wasn't planning to play, but Gin convinced me to.

She told me that my walking onto the field every Friday night for the rest of the season is like her walking back into school Wednesday morning with her face bruised and swollen. It was proof that we won't be brought down by all this—that we're stronger than that.

So here I am, dressing for a game against Mercer, hoping Jack can see from my glare across the visitors' locker room that I'd rather kick *his* ass than the other team's tonight.

I can't fucking believe he's playing tonight. That's the reason I tried to quit the team. He was arrested for battery and sexual assault, but his parents bailed him out and he's still allowed to come to school and be on the team until his case is settled. Only in Roper.

Innocent until proven guilty, Coach Carter said. Bullshit. I saw Gin's face after what happened, and I saw Jack's. That fucker is guilty, and he deserves to be in jail.

The school district is working with the police department, and they hired a security guard for Gin while she's at school. Her mom hired another one for when she's not at school.

I can't believe it's come to this. Gin's endured so much, all because of my brilliant fucking idea to give her that rose.

She keeps telling me it's not my fault, that change is painful for some people. Girls have been coming up to her at school and telling her they're sorry for not supporting her before and that they do now.

It's something.

"Get your heads out of your asses, boys!" Coach Carter yells. "It's game time. We have to leave all the drama and baggage in this locker room. Out on that field, we're one. We're a team."

I narrow my eyes at him, because rape isn't "drama."

Now that I'm seeing things through Gin's eyes, I get it. The things we'd say and do to excuse our shit behavior. The glossing over it by our coach, parents, and even teachers. That whole "I don't want to know" attitude.

All of it—bullshit.

When it's time, I put my helmet on and lead the team onto the field. It's not for them, I remind myself. Not for my worthless father. Not for myself. I'm here for Gin. If she can get through what she did, I can sure as hell do this.

We have a rocky start, to say the least. Everything just feels off tonight. I'm not paying attention to pre-snap reads. I'm sluggish and unfocused. It's all I can do not to drop the fucking ball, plow into Jack, and smash my fist into his already-smashed-up nose.

Gin told the cops it was her who broke his nose so I wouldn't get in trouble. Jack didn't say different. And everyone in school thinks she's a badass.

Mercer scores on us in the first quarter. No matter how loud Coach yells in my face, I just can't make myself care. The whole "win at any cost" attitude is what got us where we are, and I'm done with all that.

But then they score again in the second quarter. Some of my throws are good, some are off, but none of them is enough. We're down 14–0 at the half.

Our side of the stands is deathly quiet as we jog past to the locker room. I sink onto a bench and bury my face in my hands.

"What in the actual fuck is going on?" Coach Carter kicks over a folding chair, and it clatters loudly over the tile floor. "It's like watching a fucking powder-puff team!"

"I can't catch bad throws," Jack says, throwing his arms in the air.

I scowl at him. "You can't seem to catch good ones either."

"Chase, you've got no reason to be making bad throws tonight," Coach says. "This is Mercer. Fucking *Mercer*. They're probably having a circle jerk in their locker room right now over this score."

I sigh heavily, the desire to win ingrained deep inside me, like it or not.

"My ribs are sore as shit," I say. "And my shoulder. The line doesn't seem to give a shit about protecting me tonight."

Coach turns to the offensive line players. "If any player in this room wouldn't lay down on the field and let a motherfucking semi run over you to protect Chase, get out of here right now. I won't tolerate you letting personal bullshit get in the way of this team."

No one moves.

"Sorry, Chase," Sam Stockwell says. "I left you open in the second quarter, but it wasn't on purpose."

"Get. Your. Shit. Together," Coach says. "All of you."

We come out strong in the third quarter, scoring right away. I'm imagining Gin is watching from the stands, cheering for me. We tie the game at fourteen at the start of the fourth quarter, but Mercer kicks a field goal and takes a 17–14 lead.

Time seems to stop near the end of the game. My shoulder is so sore that I overthrow a pass and Jack dives for it, but it bounces off his hands and gets intercepted.

And then as the clock counts down to zero, I have to watch from the bench as the other team snaps one play and the quarterback takes a knee. My heart is in my throat as the scoreboard timer hits zero.

Zero.

It's over.

We lost.

twenty-three

Gin

IT TAKES ALMOST THREE WEEKS for my face to heal. And when I look in the mirror that first morning after every bruise has healed, I see a different girl looking back at me.

I've been hurt and scared before, but never like I was that day in the locker room. I survived, though, and I was braced to survive the aftermath too. I figured there would be more harassment after, because I'd be perceived as screwing with the Roper status quo yet again.

Not this time, though. There were stares and whispers the day after, but the anger that had been directed at me pretty much disappeared. People saw my beaten face, heard what Jack had tried to do to me, and decided enough was enough.

Girls have come up to me since and thanked me for what I've done. Even guys look at me with something new. I don't know if it's respect or just neutrality, but it's better than before.

There's a girl with wiser eyes looking back at me now. She's a few pounds thinner, because her jaws ached so badly it was hard to eat solid foods for a while.

Still, I sipped my protein shakes in the cafeteria every day, my head held high and my security guard conspicuously nearby at another table. The day I returned to school, Chase was waiting at my lunch table. He's sat beside me every day since, Lauren glaring at him most of the time.

We're here, though. Still standing. Finding a way through this new normal at Roper High School.

There have been parent-teacher meetings, teacher-student meetings, school administration-teacher meetings and parent-student-teacher-administration meetings since I was attacked. We've all talked openly about the Sweet Sixteen, and it's been made clear that anyone who does anything like that again will be expelled.

There was a lot of pressure on both sides. A regional women's advocacy group wanted every football player investigated and charged with assault if they'd taken part. The football-program-loving good-old-boy network pushed for a clean slate, fresh start approach. No one gets charged for anything that happened in the past, but moving forward, they will be.

Except for Jack. The prosecutor charged him with sexual assault, and no one objected to that.

Eventually, we all accepted the second proposal. I didn't want to see Chase's future ruined over it, because he's been beside me in every way since Jack attacked me. And I'm starting to realize the problems at our school didn't come so much from individuals, but from a culture that worshiped football and thought that consent was a black-and-white, yes-or-no issue.

Chase and I have been spending as much time together as we can. He helped me finish painting and building the play set, and he comes home with me for dinner most nights.

On Saturdays, we binge-watch shows on Netflix and cook. Chase decided that should be my mom's day off from cooking, so we come up with something each week to cook for her. Ever my mother, she asks me for a list midweek and has the groceries delivered for us.

We've gotten comfortable with each other. Confessed truths. Listened. In a very short time, Chase has become my best friend.

I'm moving Ellie's bedroom wall into place for play rehearsal four days before opening night when suddenly, it gets lighter. I turn and see Chase grinning at me, now doing most of the work.

"Thanks," I say, tucking my hair behind my ear as we set it down. "Don't you have practice?"

He grins. "I'm on my way."

The football team has won the past three games. The Mercer loss was part of the rock-bottom moment we all seemed to experience together.

The ground was pulled out from under Roper after the attack. The football program this town takes so much pride in was exposed to be imperfect. The players, human. Some of them, flawed. Others, embarrassments.

And the worst part, in the eyes of many proud former players for the team? The loss. They're still breaking down the Mercer game in coffee shops all over town.

There's no hope for some of those guys, like Chase's father. But I think we can help the younger guys learn a new way. Maybe not all of them, but some, at least.

In a twist of irony, or more likely karma, Jack is now the one under attack at school. People call him "Jack the Raper." It pisses me off that some people see everything as a game—every decision a weighing of two things to see which one is more popular. Before, the Sweet Sixteen was cool. But the tables have turned, so now lots of people say they never thought it was a good idea.

"Where's Madison?" Mr. Douglas calls out across the theater, his voice echoing through the space. "She was supposed to be on stage in her first costume almost fifteen minutes ago."

"You didn't hear?" the lighting tech, Caroline, says. "She fell in gym class and messed up her ankle. She's at the hospital."

Mr. Douglas puts his hands in his already-crazy hair and pulls. "What? The hospital? We open in four days!"

Caroline shrugs. "Maybe she's fine, I don't know."

"Well, someone call her and find out." He shakes his head and rubs his temple. "Okay, where's Grace?"

Madison's understudy, a junior, looks up from the textbook she had her face buried in while sitting in front of the stage. "What? Me?"

"Are you ready to take over for Madison if we need you? We'll have to get all the costumes re-fitted."

Grace's mouth drops open. "What? No! Like, the entire part? No, I just took the understudy thing so I'd have something for college applications."

Mr. Douglas grimaces. "Well, we'd better hope Madison's okay, or else there's no play."

Aiden, our Prince Charming, has a stunned expression that sums up everyone's mood as the theater falls into silence. I've spent three hours a day building and painting this set since school started, and so have the other crew members.

"She has a broken ankle," Caroline announces.

No one says a word. We all look at Mr. Douglas, who sighs heavily.

"Guys, I'm so sorry, but I think we have to call it off."

"That's not fair!" Evelyn, our fairy godmother, is on the verge of tears. "All because she flaked out?" She points at Grace.

Mr. Douglas puts out his hands in a calming gesture. "Let's not place blame. This is an unfortunate reality sometimes, because stuff happens. Maybe we can put on the play in the spring, but right now, we have no one who knows Ellie's part and has two functioning legs."

"What about Gin?" Chase's deep voice sounds across the theater.

I turn to face him, shocked. "What?"

"What?" Mr. Douglas echoes, his face scrunched in confusion.

Everyone turns to Chase.

"She knows all the lines," he says. "She knows that part better than Madison. I hear her telling Madison the parts she misses all the time."

My face flushes at the suggestion.

"Is that true, Gin? Do you know all the lines?"

"I mean . . . I guess I do, but . . . you don't want me. I'd be awful."

"Awful is better than no play," Aiden says hopefully.

"Better for *you*," I say, laughing humorlessly. "I'm the one who'd be humiliated." I shoot a death glare at Chase. "This is a terrible idea."

"You'd be great," he says, still digging my hole.

"Okay, no." I put my hands up, shutting down the plan he's hatching. "Ellie is a happy blonde, not a goth-looking, reclusive artist."

"But . . . can't you lose the black hair color by Saturday night?" Mr. Douglas asks.

"I don't know the first thing about acting!"

"I'll run lines with you nonstop until we open," Aiden offers. "Just do this, Gin. We've put so much work into this."

I scowl at Chase, who gives me an innocent look.

"My mom's a great seamstress," he says. "If the costumes would need to be altered."

Mr. Douglas nods, looking at me. "We have every costume here except the one for the ball. Madison was planning to bring one of her prom dresses for that."

"Okay, then it's not gonna work," I say, starting to panic. "Because I don't even have *a* prom dress, let alone multiple ones."

"I've got one you can borrow," Grace offers.

I turn to her and narrow my eyes; she gives me a sheepish smile.

"It's ultimately up to you, Gin," Mr. Douglas says. "You're our only hope at this point."

"Oh, great." I roll my eyes and throw my hands in the air. "Put that under my name in the program. *Gin Fielding—the only hope.*"

Aiden pumps his fist in the air. "She's talking about the program, which means she's saying yes!"

The whole cast and crew cheer, and I cover my face, sneaking another glare at Chase, who's cheering too, and also looking quite proud of himself.

As if I haven't been the talk of this school enough already this year, now I'm going to be known as the girl who fumbled her lines or tripped and fell off the stage with hundreds of people looking on.

So much for my low-key senior year.

twenty-four

Chase

ANDERSON CLARK LOOKS LIKE HE might piss his pants before the game even starts. Our new starting wide receiver is a sophomore who didn't expect to fill this role on the varsity team this season.

"You good?" I ask him, patting his shoulder pad.

He nods, but his eyes are wide with terror.

"You got this," I tell him. "Don't let any one play reset your mood, okay? Good or bad. You catch the ball, you drop the ball, we score, we don't—keep your head in the same place no matter what goes down."

"Is that what you do?"

"Yep. I don't think about what I've done right or wrong till the game's in the books. Keep your mind in the present at all times."

"Okay. I'll try."

There won't be any more easy wins for our team this year, but I've never been prouder to be the captain. After an outcry from some parents, Jack was suspended from the team pending the outcome of his court case, and since the case won't close out until the season is over, he's done. When he was booted, Sam Stockwell quit in protest. He tried to come back to the team a few days later, but Coach Carter told him he couldn't. The tide has turned on the Sweet Sixteen—no one wants to condone that shit anymore.

Without two of our key players in place, we've had to buckle down hard to win the last three games. I respect my coach for not letting Sam back on even though he's one of our best players and his coaching job is in jeopardy.

It's Roper, after all—the buzz about replacing him started after we lost one game.

I'm not planning on losing any more, though. Tonight's game will be extra sweet because my dad's pissed as fuck right now in the stands.

I left the locker room a few minutes ago to track him down and deliver some news right on the old Roper home field he won so many games on.

"What's up?" he asked as I approached.

"Hey, just wanted to let you know I called the Penn State coach today and committed. He wants to have a photo op of me signing with them, and I told him it'll be me, Mom, Cassie, and Alyssa."

He reared back as though I'd hit him. "You little shit. This is the thanks I get for all these years of busting my ass to make you into the player you are?"

"I'm *nothing* like you. You're a mean, washed-up drunk who beats on your wife 'cause you're not man enough to take on someone who hits back."

I'd left him standing there in stunned silence, his surrounding buddies looking equally shocked.

Fuck him. It was conversations with Gin that made me realize Penn State is right for me. I like the coach there best because he's tough but respected. He was able to tell me exactly how he sees me fitting into his program. And I think, given the recent sexual abuse there, that I can offer insight into more than just football. Maybe help some guys learn from my mistakes.

When I lead the team onto the field, I glance up into the stands and see my mom standing there in her well-worn "Roper Football Mom" sweatshirt, her expression bright and happy.

I hope she's proud of me for making my own choice about college, though I know she'll be too scared to say so if she is.

Right after kickoff, I'm totally engrossed in a play when I notice players looking over at the visiting team's bleachers. I glance over and don't see anything, but then I realize it's not about what they're *doing*, but what they're *saying*.

Roper Rapists. They're chanting it.

The sound of them making something so painful for our town, and especially for Gin, into a football game chant makes me see red. I suddenly don't just want to win this game; I want to crush it.

Anderson's more ready than he thought. He catches every good pass I throw to him, and most of them are very good. My offensive line does its job, I do mine, and Anderson does his. We win the game 35–14.

As soon as I walk out of the shower in the locker room, towel around my waist, Coach Carter approaches me.

"Just heard the news. Penn State's lucky to get you."

"Thanks."

"Boys!" he calls out. "Everyone congratulate our quarterback, who's gonna be signing with Penn State next week."

Most of the guys congratulate me. Clay Houser doesn't say a damn word. He actually looks pissed, which is bullshit. We've been playing football together since we were little kids.

"What, you don't like Penn State?" I ask him as we're both getting dressed.

His jaw tenses. "I just don't know how you managed to stay the golden boy. You were first with more of those girls than any of us. Always the MVP. And because you've got a hard-on for Gin Fielding, you're out and you come out looking like a hero. The rest of us are the bad guys."

I shake my head and run a hand through my damp hair. "No one thinks I'm any different from the rest of you in what we did. And I do feel a lot of guilt for being the one to pass out those roses. For being the first one."

"Not too guilty to take a full ride and end up getting drafted." He slams his locker door shut.

"This isn't about the Sweet Sixteen, man. You're pissed Penn State still wants me, and no place wants you."

He turns and glares at me. "Watch it, Matthews."

"Quit being a dick, then."

He steps toward me, eyes narrowed. "Yeah, I'm pissed about it. You'll move on and keep being the golden boy, while the rest of us stay here to be known as the Roper Fucking Rapists for the rest of our lives."

"No one's making you stay," I say with a shrug.

"You ruined my senior year. You were supposed to be my brother, and you blew up this team."

Others are listening to us now, but I don't care. I've thought about this a lot since Gin set things in motion, and I know he's right. I'm more responsible than the rest of the guys. It's more my fault than anyone's that we dropped that game to Mercer. I owe apologies to a lot of people, but not the ones Clay thinks.

"It needed blowing up, man," I say, ending the conversation.

There's a party after the game at a freshman's house, with music, bowls of snacks, and rows of canned soda. Kid's trying too hard, but the effort's nice.

Coach was adamant with us that we'll be kicked off the team for even being at a party with booze or sex, whether we're taking part or not. Our team has a shattered reputation to rebuild.

Ben Hart, the junior in a boot due to his foot injury, walks up to me as soon as I come into the kitchen to get a drink.

"Hey, man, congrats on Penn State," he says with a nervous smile.

"Thanks."

"Someday I'll be able to watch you playing on TV and say I knew you when."

I scoff at that. "I've got a long way to go."

"You're gonna make it. I know you will."

"Thanks, man, I appreciate that. And if you want to come hang out with me next year, catch a game, you're always welcome."

He grins. "Me?"

"Yeah, you."

"Cool." His voice cracks, and he clears his throat. "Cool, thanks."

"When you getting that boot off?"

He looks down at it. "Hopefully in three weeks."

"So you won't miss the whole season?"

"No, I'll be back to warming the bench soon." He laughs awkwardly.

"Never know when you'll get your shot," I tell him. "Someone else could get injured and open up a starting spot for you."

I think of Gin, who went to New York with her mom today to get her hair done and get a dress for the play. Her mom was so happy about her starring role that she insisted on a day off school to go to New York, make a quick stop by her publishing house, and get Gin ready for tomorrow.

A girl comes up to us, and I duck out, giving Ben an opening. There's only one girl I want to talk to anyway. I find a quiet spot in the backyard and text her.

Me: Are you back? We won. This gorgeous girl once suggested I celebrate winning with pizza, want to meet me somewhere?

Gin: We just got in half an hour ago. I'd love to, but I've been up since 4 am and I'm exhausted.

Gin: And gorgeous, you say? Will you still think she's gorgeous if her hair is the color of an orange tabby cat?

Me: I will. Seriously, you changed your hair color?

Gin: Mr. Douglas wanted me to have my natural color.

Me: Send me a pic.

Gin: Ugh, not yet. I need more time to accept how closely I resemble The Little Mermaid now.

Me: You want to watch our show and cook tomorrow?

Gin: I do, but I'm running lines with the rest of the cast all day to help me get ready.

Me: Are you still as nervous as you were yesterday?

Gin: Worse. I threw up on the plane ride home.

Me: You'll be great.

Gin: You're still coming, right?

Me: Are you kidding? I'll be in the front row.

Gin: Congrats on winning tonight. I'm still mad at you, though.

Me: That's okay, you're cute when you're mad.

Gin: Goodnight, Chase.

Me: Night. See you tomorrow.

"WHAT'S WITH THE BUCKET?" MR. Douglas asks me with a frown.

"Oh." I glance down at the blue plastic two-gallon pail I'm clutching the handle of, and then give him a sheepish smile. "You know, in case of vomiting."

"Vomiting? Are you *that* nervous?"

I nod. "I'm beyond nervous. If you happen to have a sedative in your pocket, this would be a great time to give it to me."

"Gin. Listen to me. I've been watching you run these lines all day, and you're . . . you've got this part locked up." He looks from side to side. "If you'd auditioned for this part, I would have cast you."

"Really?" I pretty much squeak.

"Absolutely. Just stay focused on your lines and pretend we're rehearsing one more time in an empty theater. Forget about the audience."

Just the word "audience" makes my stomach roll with nausea. It would be one thing if I had to do this in front of a bunch of strangers, but my mom and Michael are out there watching. Chase. Raj and Lauren. If I humiliate myself, I'll be doing it in front of everyone I know.

Everyone's running around fussing over last-minute stuff. Harrison, the junior who's doing the makeup tonight, comes up to look me over one more time. He applies more light pink lipstick and dabs a tissue to my chin and nose.

"I feel like a clown," I say, sighing.

"That's because you don't usually wear makeup." He scowls at me. "That black crayon you line your eyes with doesn't count."

"Yeah, but . . . isn't this too dramatic a change? From nothing to—" I gesture in front of my face in a circular motion "—this?"

He crosses his arms over his chest. "Like I already said, you look gorgeous. Your skin is to die for, and now that your brows are shaped and your hair is back to its natural color, it's like looking at a different person."

"But it's so much makeup, Harrison."

Rolling his eyes, he repeats what he's been telling me for the past hour. "The stage lights wash you out. You have to wear more for it to look average on stage. Will you just trust me?"

"I'm trying," I say weakly.

"Did I come hover over your sets and ask if that paint shade was right?"

I sigh heavily. "No."

"This is because I'm a guy, isn't it? You assume all guys only do drag queen makeup?"

"No! I didn't say anything like that."

He puts his hands on my shoulders. "Gin, relax. I get it. You're used to blending in, but for the next two hours, you're gonna stand out. Like it or not."

"Not," I admit, cringing. "I still can't believe Chase did this to me."

Harrison scrunches his face and mocks crying. "Poor Gin. She's rich, and the golden boy follows her around like a lost puppy with emoji heart eyes. And she's a natural redhead."

"Places!" Mr. Douglas calls out.

Harrison puts a hand on the handle of my bucket, tugging at it. "Gin, let go."

"But . . . I need it."

"You can't take a bucket on stage with you." He pulls harder, taking it from me, and I feel truly naked.

My first costume is ragged clothes from Goodwill, and this is the one I'm most comfortable in. I take my place, reminding myself that the sooner the play starts, the sooner it will be over.

When the curtains open, I remember Mr. Douglas's words. I pretend we're just rehearsing again. I don't look at the audience at all. Even if I seem to be looking at them, I'm not.

Once I get the first five minutes behind me, I start to relax. When Ellie faces bullies at school, I channel my own feelings from the past six weeks. As she confesses her love for Prince Charming, I picture Chase.

At some point that I can't even put my finger on, I start having fun. I know this part well. With every laugh, every smile over my shoulder, I become Ellie rather than Gin.

Ellie is a daydreamer who doesn't think she's anything special. I'm the opposite—a practical realist who knows she belongs somewhere bigger and broader than Roper, Missouri. But as I see through Ellie's eyes, I start to think that maybe I could be more like her. Maybe I should.

I become so focused on my delivery that I stop keeping track of time. I want to do Ellie justice.

In the kissing scene Aiden and I only practiced once, he honors my wish and kisses me beside my lips rather than on them. I've never had a real kiss, and I didn't want my first one to be with him, in front of an audience.

By the time I have to walk onstage in the long, sleeveless emerald gown my mom and I picked out at a New York boutique yesterday, I'm not nervous anymore. With the smooth, shiny red hair it took six hours in a hair salon to get and this beautiful dress I let my mom talk me into, I'm not the Gin I was before.

If nothing else, *I did this*, and I'm proud of myself for that. I stepped into a leading role I never thought I'd have to play, and because of me, we didn't have to cancel the show.

It's easier to be brave than vulnerable. Standing on the principles my mom taught me was easier than this was. In black eyeliner and baggy clothes, I send a message that I'm above style and completely unconcerned with what anyone thinks.

But tonight, I'm on stage. Lights are shining on me. Everyone is looking. I'm asking them to not just see me as playing a pretty, would-be princess, but to believe I could actually be one.

That's raw in a way I've never allowed. And by the end of the play, I have tears in my eyes because I'm so damn proud that I put myself out there.

We soak in the applause. And as we all stand there listening to the cheers of approval, I finally look into the audience.

And there he is. Chase is in the front row, as promised. He's wearing a light blue dress shirt and khakis, and he's beaming. No one is clapping louder or cheering harder. His gaze never leaves me. I smile back, knowing he was right to push me into this role. He believed in me more than I believed in myself.

My mom and Michael are just a couple rows behind him. Even from the stage, I can see that my mom is crying. Michael passes her a tissue, and I get a premonition that Michael is soon to be more than the caretaker of our house. It makes me happy.

Once backstage, I'm mobbed with hugs and congratulations. When one person finishes hugging, another takes over. Even Madison greets me from her crutches.

"Hey," she says. "Cute dress."

"Thanks."

That's as close as I'm getting to congratulations from her. I can tell she's crushed she didn't get to play Ellie, and I understand that.

My mom finds me and passes me two dozen calla lilies. Michael holds them as she crushes me in a hug, whispering tearfully in my ear.

"I've never been so proud. I can't stop crying. I know I'm making a fool of myself, but I can't stop."

My eyes fill with tears as she talks. I love her so much. I can't imagine not seeing her every day anymore. I thought leaving Roper would only be sweet, but there will be some bitter mixed in too.

When Mom pulls away to mop her cheeks again, Michael hands me the lilies with a smile. But as soon as Mom sees Chase rushing my way, she grabs them back out of my arms.

Chase is grinning like never before. He passes me a dozen pale pink carnations with tissue paper wrapped around the bunch, then sweeps me into his powerful embrace, lifting my feet from the floor as he spins me around.

"You were amazing, Gin," he says in my ear. "I'm blown away."

"I can't believe I did it."

"I can."

I just hold on to him, taking in the solid feel of his broad back beneath my arms and the brush of his hair against my cheek.

"Thank you for the flowers," I say in his ear. "They're beautiful."

"I'll never give you another rose again," he says in a low tone.

He sets me back on the ground, locks his eyes on mine, and cups my face in his large hands.

We're surrounded by people, but we might as well be the only ones in the world. I can't hear, see, or feel anything but Chase as he leans down to kiss me.

His lips are a soft contrast to the slight stubble on his face. My heart flips and flops, scrambling to find its pace again. The kiss is only a couple seconds long, but it carries a promise of more to come. The heat in Chase's eyes vows the next one won't be so sweet.

My body burns with desire for him. This is the best day of my life. I got to play a character who got her Prince Charming, and my real-life one is kissing me backstage.

Chase leans in to say something in my ear.

"Please don't change your hair back, I love it."

I smile, a flush creeping up my neck to my face.

"Okay, I'll keep it."

"Also, I'm gonna need to take you out on a date."

I pull back and look at him, brows arched. "A date?"

He nods. "As soon as possible. Right now would be great. You should keep the dress on."

I laugh as he leans his forehead down against mine. "I promised Mom and Michael we'd go out with them tonight. How about if we go out alone tomorrow night?"

"Deal," he says.

Everyone is looking at us. But now, the looks are happy ones. No one's judging or angry. And finally, I'm okay with them looking. My plan to stay unseen this year was a fail, but I'm pretty sure this is exactly how it was supposed to be.

twenty-six

Chase

I CAN'T STAND TO BE in my own house anymore. I slept there, and this morning, I got the hell out and I plan to stay gone as late as I can.

My mom's arm was in a sling when I saw her making coffee on my way out of the house. This time, she didn't try to tell me she fell. We both know what happened. Our eyes met across the kitchen, and I said, "I'll help you get out of here when you're ready."

Her expression was panicked as she hissed a whispered response. "Chase, don't say things like that."

I shook my head. "It's not gonna get better, Mom. It could be Cassie or Alyssa next. If you won't leave for yourself, leave for them."

"Keep talking like that, and he'll kick you out," she said.

"I don't care." I shrugged and left, spending the day working on the farm of a former Roper football player. He lets me work for him anytime I need some cash.

I went back home late in the afternoon for a shower, and then walked to Milano's, the Italian place in downtown Roper where I'm meeting Gin.

She gives me a pointed look as soon as she walks in the front door and sees me. I slide out of the booth I'm sitting in and stand up, greeting her with a hug and a kiss on the cheek.

"Why wouldn't you let me pick you up?" she asks. "Did you walk here?"

"Look, it's bad enough I can't pick you up for our first date because I don't have a car. I'm sure as hell not letting you pick me up."

"So what if you don't have a car?" She shakes her head in frustration. "Next time, just let me drive, okay?"

"Yeah." I grin at her, not willing to start out our date with an argument. "You look great."

"Oh." She puts a hand on her hair, which is loose around her shoulders. "Thanks."

She's wearing dark jeans, brown boots, and a green sweater. I've been attracted to Gin for a while now, but seeing her like this—looking fresh and confident—brings it to a new level.

We order sodas and a pizza to share, and as soon as the waitress leaves the table, Gin gives me a secret smile.

"What?" I ask.

"I listened to your game online the other night."

"Oh yeah?"

She holds my gaze across the table. "I've never really gotten football. The excitement people feel when watching it, I mean. But I was getting into it. Every time you threw a complete pass, I was . . . proud of you."

She looks down sheepishly. I reach across the table and take her hand.

"Hey, look at me," I say. "I can't tell you how great that makes me feel. Of all the people in the world I want to be proud of me, you're at the very top."

"I am?"

"Of course. I'm crazy about you, Gin. You know that."

"Well, I mean . . . I figured there was something, because . . . the kiss and all . . ."

I stroke my thumb over her knuckles. "So, hey . . . I'm wondering something." I clear my throat and square my shoulders. "Even though I've done stuff I'm not proud of and I can think of a hundred reasons I don't deserve you, I want to be with you. When I saw you on stage with Aiden last night, I had this primal urge to beat the shit out of him and throw you over my shoulder."

She arches her brows in amusement. "That would have stolen the show."

"Yeah. Point is, I'm working on being a better person now, and I was thinking, you know, that if, from here on out, I do things in a way that makes me deserve you . . . will you be with me?"

Her lips part with surprise. "You mean like . . . in the future?"

"I mean right now."

"Oh." A slow smile creeps across her pretty face. "Yes, I'd like that."

"I've never been in a relationship with just one girl. But since things started with us, I can't even look at anyone else. You're the only one I want."

The waitress brings our sodas, and Gin lets go of my hand so she can put a straw in her Sprite.

"When did things start for us, for you?" she asks.

I think about it as I take a drink of my Coke. "I guess . . . that time I saw you at the Y. What about you?"

She laughs. "You know . . . third grade?"

"But you liked other guys in there too, right?"

"No. I've had a hardcore crush on you for a long time."

"I never knew." I take her hand again. "I mean, you mentioned before that you had a crush on me, and I've thought about it, but you never let on."

"I would have been mortified for you to know. For anyone to know."

"Why?"

"Because . . ." She shrugs. "You were out of my league."

I shake my head. "No . . . you were out of mine. But I realized when I saw you with Aiden last night that I'd rather become the guy you deserve than lose you to someone else."

Her smile lights up her blue eyes. "You're the only one I want, too, Chase. But I've never had a relationship either, and I don't know what I'm doing."

"We can figure it out as we go."

"Okay."

I look from side to side, making sure no one is eavesdropping before I continue.

"Look, I need you to know that I'm not going to try to sleep with you. I've spent a lot of time thinking about it, and I need to stay away from that altogether for a while. A long time. After what I've done, there's no way I'd feel right about being with you. If we get there, I want it to mean something. For both of us."

"Good. I feel the same way. I'm nowhere near ready for that."

I sigh deeply. "Now that we've decided that, I need to ask what you think about something."

"What's that?"

"Do you think I should apologize to the girls I . . . you know . . ."

She squeezes my hand. "I think if you're feeling like you should, you should."

"I don't even know how to begin to apologize for it. It feels shitty to just show up and say sorry and expect everything to be okay."

"Sorry doesn't mean everything's okay. It just means you care enough to own what you did and show remorse."

I nod. "That's a good way to look at it."

Gin cocks her head, forcing me to make eye contact with her. "Hey, what's on your mind right now?"

I cringe. "The number of girls I have to apologize to. God, I've been an asshole."

"Just look ahead, Chase. You can't undo any of it."

"The worst part of all of this is how much it makes me feel like my dad." Shame floods me as I look away from Gin. "He treats my mom like shit, and that's what I did to all those girls."

"You didn't have much of an example, but you figured out right and wrong for yourself."

I tighten my hold on her hand. "My mom's arm is in a sling. I guess my dad must've taken out my decision to go to Penn State on her. So that feels really shitty, too."

"I can't imagine."

"I can't wait to get the hell out of that house. I just wish I could take my mom and sisters with me."

"If they ever need a place to go, they can go to my mom's. She'll let them stay as long as they need. Will you tell your mom that?"

Reluctantly, I nod. "I appreciate it. She'll be embarrassed that you and your mom know what's going on."

"No need for that. Your dad's the one who should be embarrassed."

"Have you talked to your mom about it?"

"A little. She wanted me to tell you that you shouldn't feel guilty about any of it. That your mom can't have better until she wants better."

Our pizza comes, and we spend a minute eating in silence.

When I speak again, I say, "If I'm ever not good to you—in any way—call me out on it, okay?"

Gin smiles. "I wouldn't be able to help myself from calling you out. And same here. I know I'm not perfect."

"Yeah, but your mom's taught you how to treat people a lot better than my parents taught me."

"Hey, Chase?" Gin sets down her cup and gives me a serious look.

"Hmm?"

"If we're doing this relationship thing, which I totally think we should do, it's between you and me, okay? I don't want us worrying about shit like whose parents are worse and who has a car."

"Yeah, okay."

A few people I know from school come into the restaurant. They wave at us and sit at a booth nearby, the girls eyeing Gin and me. I take her hand again, wanting everyone to know we're together.

"How many people have told you how great your hair looks?" I ask.

She smiles. "A few."

"You're the most beautiful girl I've ever seen."

The light pink blush that drives me crazy spreads across her face. Damn. Abstaining from sex will be hard with her nearby, but I know it's the right thing.

"So," she says in a low tone, "no sex, but we'll still do . . . other stuff, right?"

"I'll peck you on the cheek anytime you want." I wink at her.

Her expression turns skeptical. "Uh-huh."

"Yeah, we'll get to other stuff. Stop being so horny."

Gin's mouth drops open with indignation. She tosses a pepperoni across the table, and it bounces off my cheek. I pick up a black olive from my plate and throw it at her. She ducks and avoids it.

"Better work on your throwing technique," she says, laughing.

Even though things are still shit at home, I'm happier than I've ever been. Gin is everything I've ever wanted in a girl and more. For the first time in my life, I'm falling hard for someone.

Taking it slow with her is important to me. I don't want to fuck this up. And when we do decide to sleep together, I want her to know it's not about getting laid. I want so much more than that with her.

More dates. More Saturdays at her house. More late-night text convos. More everything.

With Gin, it's always been more.

twenty-seven

Gin

Two Months Later

THE BLEACHERS AT THE ROPER High School stadium are packed full of people. I had no idea it would be this loud. Either the crowd is hollering, the band is playing, or the cheerleaders are yelling. And everyone is dressed in red—some people even have their faces painted red and their hair is the shade of a fire engine. For once, my red hair fits in.

It's like the entire town is here, everyone wanting to cheer Roper on to a state championship. It didn't matter that the game was more than an hour from Roper—school buses were loaded up with people of all ages for the trip. And the bus windows were filled with red "Go Roper" signs, of course.

This is everything I've always hated about Roper. The near-worship of the football program. It's put on a pedestal by most everyone in this town like nothing else.

But this time . . . I kind of don't hate it. I kind of love it.

I'm wearing one of Chase's jerseys, which he insisted on. Since it's December and it's freezing, I'm wearing a black thermal shirt beneath the jersey and a red stocking cap.

Lauren is on one side of me, and Raj is on the other. Beside him is Michelle, sitting extra close to Raj. I've never been to a football game before. I vowed I'd never go to one. But when Chase asked me to be here for the final game of his final high school football season, I said yes.

When he throws a perfect pass to Anderson for Roper's second touchdown of the game, I jump out of my seat with everyone else, screaming with excitement.

Lauren stays seated. It was all I could do to get her to wear a red hoodie to the game.

"Gin, I'm the antithesis of school spirit," she said in a deadpan voice. "Before you started dating the golden boy, you were too."

"I know. I get it, I really do. But will you please just do it—for me?"

She rolled her eyes and called me a few names as she put on the sweatshirt.

"You want me to put your hair up in a ponytail with a giant red ribbon, too?" she asked, heavy on the sarcasm. "Maybe we both should just wear cheerleading skirts."

"That's not a bad idea," I said, nodding.

"Fuck you."

What can I say? I love Lauren, rough edges and all. She's accepted that I'm with Chase pretty decently, considering. For the first couple weeks, she was extra chilly, but seeing how happy he makes me warmed her up eventually.

She still drops the occasional off-color joke about jocks, but he doesn't mind. And when he kisses me in front of her, she tells us we're more sickening than a powerful strain of Ebola, but that's just part of her charm.

"I'm freezing my tits off," she says to me in a rare quiet-ish moment of the game.

"Want me to go get a coat and gloves from my mom?" I ask her.

"I'll go."

We came to the game with Mom and Michael. Michael drove us all in his big SUV. Mom insisted they sit with the other parents, while we sat in the student section. I wasn't loving that idea, but then I saw that the student section was in front, where I could get a good view of the game.

Brittany Dively is leading the cheerleaders in a cheer on the track in front of our team's stands. Her hair is up in a ponytail with a giant bow, like Lauren was teasing me about earlier. As I watch Brittany, I think about how different I've always felt from her. She's blond and very outgoing. I swear she's in a good mood every moment of every day.

Where will life take her after this year? Will she go to a big college and be one of thousands trying to find their way? Maybe she'll stay in Roper, where she'll always be a former cheerleader, watching from the stands as younger girls bounce and yell on the sidelines.

I feel commonality with her for the first time. After we graduate, we're all headed into unknowns. We may have goals and dreams, but none of us knows for sure if we'll reach them. Life could throw any of us a curveball.

"Gin." Michelle leans across Raj to pass me a paper cup. "Hot chocolate."

"Thanks."

She smiles at Raj, who puts his arm around her. The two of them have been so good for each other. He adores her, and she trusts him. I don't know how serious they are, and I hope neither of them ends up brokenhearted, because they're both good people. But nothing is ever guaranteed.

It's halftime, and I watch as Chase pulls off his helmet on the sideline. A puff of air forms in front of his face as he exhales in the cold night air. He takes a sip of water from a paper cup someone hands him and then looks up into the stands.

He's looking for me. My heart pounds as I watch his eyes roam the crowd, trying to spot me. A few months ago, I would have thought this was impossible—even more unlikely than me going to a football game.

His gaze lands on me, and a smile spreads across his face. I grin and blush, because I can't help it when he looks at me that way. There are 1,913 people here tonight—according to the announcer, anyway—but the warmth on Chase's face makes me feel like the only one.

We've been doing a lot more than kissing recently. When we're tucked under a blanket on the couch at my house watching movies on Saturday nights, our hands roam and things usually turn heated. There was one time when Chase's shoulder was sore from a game and I didn't want to touch him there, no matter how much he told me it was okay, and things stayed PG that week.

Other weeks, though . . . we spend hours making out, discovering what touches make the other's breath catch. When Chase kisses the side of my neck, I melt. If I gently run my nails along his spine, he shudders.

The intimacy between us is like nothing I've ever felt. I didn't know a simple touch could set me off in so many ways. Chase whispers in my ear how much he loves it too, telling me no one has ever gotten to know his body like I am, and that he's never been closer to anyone.

Could sex be more intoxicating than this? Could *anything*?

Chase's coach yells out something, and he looks away, breaking the spell between us. He leads his team into the locker room, and I sigh softly, sipping my hot chocolate.

"You two are sweeter than cotton candy," Lauren grumbles as she sits down beside me. "I get a fucking cavity every time I look at you eye-fucking each other."

I look over at her and laugh. She's now wearing a gray parka, and her hair is tucked into a knitted stocking hat that says, "Go Roper" and has a big, fuzzy red ball on top.

"Yeah, so funny," she says. "Laugh it up. This is all Mama Fielding brought. She cleaned out the sporting goods store. Roper scarves, gloves, and hats for all."

I love that my mom is here, and that she's seeing Michael. I've always wanted her to have more than her books when I go away to college. This is the first time she's been part of the Roper crowd too, and I think she's liking it.

"We need a picture," I tell Lauren.

"Eat shit."

"Seriously. One picture. Come on."

She rolls her eyes but goes along, letting me take one of the two of us and another of us with Raj and Michelle. She even smiles . . . kind of.

My mom stops by our seats with hot dogs, nachos, and more hot chocolate for all of us. We eat and put blankets on our laps, warming up a little before halftime is over.

When Chase leads the team back onto the field and we're all standing and cheering, I see a few snowflakes through the bright stadium lights.

It's December, after all. My nose feels like it's Roper-red as the game starts back up, but I'm having the best time.

Roper hasn't lost a game since the Mercer one. Still, this season won't be an undefeated one. Chase said he thinks the loss has made the fans and support feel more vital. The stands have been packed past capacity since, people cheering until they're hoarse.

My voice will probably be weak after this game. The team we're playing is good, and it's not an easy win, but finally, a 27–21 victory ends the season.

There's red and white confetti everywhere. Bullhorns are sounding. People are crying. I lose track of everyone who grabs me for a hug.

I scan the field, trying to find Chase. The players are in a big pile on the field, but I spot Chase when he crawls out, laughing and pumping his fist.

It means everything to be here right now. Happy tears shine in my eyes as I look at Chase, who finally knows he's leading his team in the right direction. This win was important to him—proof that they could come back and not just be as good as before, but in some ways, better.

He looks up at me, and I morph into a mushy girlfriend, smiling and blowing him a kiss. When he gestures with his arm, waving for me to come to him, I look around me and shake my head.

I can't go down there. Everyone would see me. It's only players and coaches on the field.

He nods and gestures again. I shake my head again.

I'm expecting him to give up, but instead, he shrugs and starts walking toward me.

"Oh, hell," Lauren says under her breath. "This is about to be some 'you complete me' bullshit."

Chase jogs across the track and pulls himself up and over the metal rail in front of the bleachers. Everyone cheers as he jogs my way, a huge grin on his sweaty face.

My tears spill over when he reaches me and sweeps me into his arms. I wrap my arms around him as best I can with the shoulder pads, and he swings me around just like he did the night of the play.

He kisses me, and I cup his cheek in my hand. The crowd is still in full celebration mode. A few seconds later, his sisters both run up, and he sets me back on the ground, putting an arm around each of the girls and picking them up next.

They're so proud of him. Everyone is. In these stands, there are no colors or classes dividing anyone. Young, old, rich, poor—none of that matters tonight. We're all Roper fans.

I see it so clearly in that moment. Roper's football program means so much to so many because it gives them something to believe in. Something to be proud of.

And right now, I couldn't be prouder of our team myself. Not just Chase, but all of them. The players who are left are finding a new way forward, without sex as a reward they're entitled to.

They deserve a chance to win at it. And if they do, they'll never have a bigger fan than me.

twenty-eight

Chase

Five Months Later

"GINGER NOELLE FIELDING."

I stand up and cheer for Gin as she walks across the stage to get her diploma. Once she has it in hand, she moves her tassel to the side, finds me in the crowd of graduating seniors, and smiles.

We made it. Not that there was any doubt that we'd graduate, but the year started out rockier than planned. I never thought I'd graduate from high school with a serious girlfriend I plan to stay with, but it's Gin, so there's no other way it could've gone.

We've been together for seven months now, and I can't imagine a life without her. Going to different colleges will be a challenge, but we're determined to make it work.

When it's time for the students in my row of chairs to stand and line up by the stage, I look through the crowd in the bleachers for my family. I can't find them—the place is packed.

They're out there somewhere, though. My mom's been crying

over this day for the past week. Cassie and Alyssa brought extra tissues for her. Cassie's already started packing her stuff to move into my bedroom, because when I leave for college next month, she and Alyssa will finally have their own rooms.

I get to the front of the line, and when one of the school board members says, "Chase Paul Matthews," there are hoots and hollers from the crowd. I take my diploma, move my tassel, and walk back to my seat, the finality of it hitting me.

In a month, I'm leaving Roper. I have to be at Penn State two months before classes start because I've got football camp. I would've loved an entire summer with Gin before school starts, but we're getting a month, which is something.

Julia's taking both of us on a three-week trip to Europe in a few days as a graduation gift. Michael's coming too. I was so shocked by her generosity when she told us that I couldn't even reply for a minute.

I spend more time at Gin's house than my own, and her mom is amazing. She makes dinner for us if we're there, unless it's Saturday. That's still our night to cook. I'm gonna miss her and Michael when I leave.

After every graduate's name is called, we all throw our hats in the air in celebration. We're no longer high school students. The first thing I do is find Gin, who puts her arms around me in a tight hug.

"You're officially dating a college guy," I say, kissing her neck, then her cheek, then her lips.

"Lucky me," she says in my ear.

"Love you." I close my eyes and take in the faint coconut smell of her hair.

"Love you back." She cups my cheek.

Julia and Michael find us at the same time my family does.

My dad gives Gin and Julia the cool greeting he always does—he blames Gin for the changes in me this year and thinks Julia is a snotty rich person.

I can't wait to get the hell away from him. My mom gave him an ultimatum a couple months ago—quit drinking, or she'll leave him. He's been sober so far—I think—but I don't have faith it'll last.

My dad is who he is, and he won't change. He's selfish and mean. I didn't even want him here today, but my mom said it's important to her, so I gave in.

We all pose for photos, and then Mom and Julia need to go so they can get ready for the graduation parties they're hosting. Mine will be another thing I do for my mom's sake. I don't want to sit around with extended family and friends from our neighborhood making small talk.

"Great speech," I tell Raj.

"Thanks."

He's our class valedictorian, and I know how hard he worked to earn it. He's been stressed the entire semester about his math grades. Even though he never says it, I sense that Raj feels a responsibility to honor his late parents in everything he does. Same with his adoptive ones. He's going to be premed at Washington University, and then he wants to go to medical school to become a surgeon.

Lauren is going to community college and working. Michelle's going to University of Missouri to study journalism. I never would have gotten to know any of them if not for Gin, and I consider all of them friends now. Even though Lauren still scowls at me, Gin assures me she and I are good. Lauren scowls at pretty much everyone.

"You guys can come by my party if you want," Raj offers.

Gin looks up at me before answering. "We might later. We're doing Chase's first and then mine."

"What other parties are you guys going to tonight?" Michelle asks.

I wrap an arm around Gin and pull her against my side. "We don't know yet."

We do know, but that's something we decided to keep to ourselves. Gin and I aren't going to any other parties tonight. We're driving to St. Louis, where we got a hotel room for the night.

After seven months of heavy make-out sessions, we've decided we're ready for more. Tonight we'll have sex for the first time, and I think I'm more nervous than Gin is.

I know it'll be different with Gin. Everything is. But I want to make sure *she* knows it's different. And with it being her first time, I want it to be perfect.

I want her to be mine in every way. She can set me on fire with just a look. Make me hard with whispered promises. Even her laugh turns me on.

The hottest thing about Gin is that the sexy part of her is just for me. She doesn't flaunt it. Hell, other people have no idea how hot she really is. It's not the way her ass looks in jeans that makes me crazy, but the things we share that no one else knows about. The parts of her I'm the only man to ever see and touch.

I can't give her that part of myself. I've been with a lot of girls before her. But she's the only one I've ever loved.

It won't be easy to stay together while living states apart. She was hesitant to even try a long-distance relationship at first. But I told her it was that or I'd become a New York City bum just to be near her.

I was only half joking. I don't want to start over in college, free to sleep with women with no strings. I can't possibly give up my best friend, the first person I want to tell everything.

We'll figure it out. If this year has taught me anything, it's that having someone in my life whose happiness means more to me that my own drives me to be better.

It's ironic that the first girl to tell me no ended up becoming the only woman I want. Or maybe it's not. Gin isn't willing to settle, and I love that about her. It's probably got something to do with seeing my mom settle for so long.

I hope like hell she'll leave my dad, but I know I can't force her to.

Gin and I pose and smile for more photos, most with people who aren't close friends. Some are with my teammates. Most of those friendships never recovered from the Sweet Sixteen fallout, but a few did.

"I'm starving," Gin says on the walk back to her car.

"We're eating as soon as we get there. My mom went a little overboard with the food."

She smiles. "Overboard sounds perfect."

I watch as she takes off her graduation cap and shakes out her fiery red hair. I'm already thinking about getting my hands in it tonight. I'll have to stop myself from getting rough with her, though my desire is pent-up to a point I feel shaky sometimes.

There'll be time for that. I've never been with anyone enough times to know them inside out. I want that with Gin. After seven months, I already know quite a lot about her.

Her inner thighs are ticklish. She loves having her neck kissed, especially on the sides. Her nipples are so sensitive I can get her close to coming just by playing with them.

Thinking about her is making me hard, and I can't hide that well with this damn red robe on, so I shift my thoughts to our vacation.

"Are you all packed yet?" I ask her as she drives us to my parents' house.

She laughs. "Not even close. How about you?"

"Just about."

"Are you still crazy excited about tonight?"

This time, it's me who laughs. "Yeah, that's one way to put it."

"You're nervous."

"A little," I admit. "But mostly just wound tight. You're my fantasy, you know? I hope it's as good for you as I know it will be for me."

She pats my knee, bringing back my hard-on. "I have no doubt, babe."

I bring her hand to my lips and kiss her knuckles. "Is it bad that I never want you to be with another guy? Ever?"

Gin glances at me and smiles. "No. I don't want you to be with anyone else ever again either."

"You're the only one I want."

After a deep breath, she says, "Then let's go enjoy these graduation parties so we can get to tonight."

I squeeze her hand, ready not just for tonight, but more. Gin saw me at my worst in the past. She knows I'm trying to make amends be a better man now. I know the best is yet to come, not just for me, but for us.

epilogue

Gin

Five Years Later

MORNING SUNLIGHT STREAMS INTO THE bedroom, and I know without even looking at the clock that this is the time I'd normally be waking up.

I'd be showering, drying my hair, and then eating a sesame seed bagel with avocado on my way out the door to Morris Carver Middle School. And then I'd spend my day teaching kids how to draw, paint, and sculpt, while also answering questions about everything from where pimples come from to why my hair is red.

I'm a middle school art teacher. I didn't see that coming. But at NYU, I discovered that while I love art and acting, my true passion is teaching. So now, a sprawling middle school is like a second home to me.

But not today. Not for the next three months, actually. I'm officially on summer break.

I burrow under the covers and wrap myself around Chase's warm, hard body, making a low, humming sound of satisfaction.

He kisses my forehead, then my cheeks, then my nose. I still think I could go back to sleep, until I feel his lips on my neck. I shiver, breaking out in goose bumps as I become as warm on the inside as I am on the outside.

"Mmm, Chase." I thread my fingers into his short golden blond hair.

"You're awake," he says softly against my skin. "Good."

"Uh-huh. Because who wants to sleep in on the first day of summer break?"

"Not us." There's a smile in his deep voice. "Hey, look around."

He pulls the covers down from my face, and I open my eyes. I gasp and cover my mouth with a hand when I see.

Our bedroom is *filled* with pink carnations. The dresser, shelves, and side tables are all lined with vases of them. There must be fifty dozen flowers in here.

"Chase." I turn to my husband. "What the . . . ?"

"Happy anniversary, babe."

I kiss him, not caring about morning breath. One year ago today, we exchanged wedding vows in the backyard of my mom's house. I knew we'd go to dinner tonight and exchange gifts, but I wasn't expecting anything like this.

"When did you do this?" I ask him.

"After you fell asleep last night."

I look at the carnations surrounding us again. "It's amazing. Thank you." I launch myself at him, and he laughs softly as I wrap myself around him.

"You deserve ten thousand carnations for putting up with me," he says with a smile.

"At least." I put my hands on his cheeks and kiss him. "But this will do. And you're not so bad, Matthews."

Chase is everything I ever wanted and so much more. Seattle

drafted him, so that's where we live now. He gets busy during the season, but he always makes time for date nights. When he's out of town for a game and I can't go because of work, he has dinner delivered to our apartment to make sure I get a good meal. Of course, he takes credit for cooking that night, and I let him, because I take credit for cooking on taco night, and that's not actually much work.

"I don't know how we got through living apart for four years," he says, running his fingertips down my cheek.

"Me either," I murmur, his blue eyes as mesmerizing to me now as they were when I lusted after him from afar growing up.

"You're all mine this month."

"I can't wait."

He runs the tip of his thumb over my lips, and I close my eyes. I love every moment we have together, but waking up together is my favorite. In New York, I missed him so much, it was a physical ache sometimes. We FaceTimed and spent as many weekends together as we could, but it never felt like enough. Our lives were in separate places.

We made it, though. It was during a summer visit home to Roper between our sophomore and junior years that Chase proposed to me on a quiet summer night at the football stadium. He told me the Sweet Sixteen will always be full of dark memories for him, except for the way it brought us together.

He was sheepish about only having a simple silver band—the best he could afford at the time—but that band was and is perfect. It's all I wear to this day to symbolize our marriage.

Even now, we live beneath our means. We have a nice, modern apartment that lets in as much light as the rainy Seattle weather will allow, but it's nothing fancy. It's June, which we've been looking forward to all year, and we're road-tripping with Chase's sisters and then spending a week alone in Hawaii. His parents are still together, and we see them briefly on holidays, but it's always awkward and uncomfortable. It hurts Chase that his mother didn't take his offer to move her into her own place. We hold out hope that maybe someday she'll want better for herself.

Chase likes to save money. We're focused on that and putting his sisters through school. For us, a splurge is dinner at a really nice restaurant or a new piece of furniture. Some of Chase's teammates run through their money buying jewelry and cars, but that's not us.

We're still two kids from Roper in some ways. And time and distance have shown me that Roper, while imperfect, isn't as bad as I thought. They've come a long way since banishing the Sweet Sixteen.

We keep up on things at Roper High School since Alyssa goes there. At least, she did until graduating last month. The school administration implemented a mandatory class for freshmen on sexual health, with a strong emphasis on consent.

"So what now?" I ask Chase playfully. "Should we go out for breakfast?"

He narrows his eyes and grabs my ass. "Food? You're thinking about food right now?"

"You know me—always hungry."

His next kiss is deeper and longer. "Always hungry, huh? What can I do to satisfy you?"

I run my hands over his shoulders and arms, the ridges of hard muscle warm beneath my fingers. I've never wanted another man; it's always been Chase for me. Even when I thought he'd never notice me. Even when I scornfully rejected him. Even when I was surrounded by other guys in New York. He'll always be my one and only.

"You know what I like, babe," I murmur against his neck.

He trails his hand up my outer thigh, his fingertips skimming beneath the seam of my panties. Within minutes, we're celebrating our anniversary with early morning lovemaking I'll be thinking of all day long. Hands fist sheets and moans fill the room.

My husband incites my desire like nothing else ever has. If we're together, I want to be close to him, whether we're in bed or just watching a movie. His touch is my comfort and my undoing; he's the only one who can both soothe me and set me aflame with need.

I don't know if it will always be like this. I can't imagine staying this deeply in love for our entire lives. We had ups and downs in college—there was even one time we talked about breaking up.

We couldn't do it, though. Losing Chase would have devastated me. On our wedding day, we promised to stay true to each other through whatever life brings our way.

That's the beauty of all-in love. It's having someone you know will be there for the bad times. When you're ugly crying and being irrational. Anyone can stay through the sexy, fun parts.

But Chase has always loved me most when I'm the most unlovable. He's my other half. Somehow, that rose that represented everything I hate ended up bringing me together with the man I love so deeply it hurts sometimes.

Some days, our love is the velvety, brilliantly colored petals of a rose. Other days, it's the piercing, ugly thorns.

I'll take both, though. I couldn't appreciate the petals if not for the thorns.

author's note

THANK YOU FOR READING SWEET Sixteen! This book was a different turn for me and I loved writing it. If you're inclined to write a review, I'd appreciate it so much.

You can discover my other books and find my social media links at www.brendarothert.com.

acknowledgements

THIS BOOK STARTED TO TAKE shape in my head more than a year ago. Though I started writing it immediately, I needed time for the characters and story to evolve in my mind before I was able to finish.

Chase and Gin mean a great deal to me. Chase, because he admits his wrongs and tries to atone for them. And Gin, just for being Gin. There's more of me in Gin than in any heroine I've ever written. That feeling of being different, apart from the crowd, was something I struggled with at her age, too.

My amazing bookish tribe helped with this book in more ways than I can put into words, but words are required here, so I'll have to do my best.

KP Simmon and Rachel VanDyken each took time to sit down with me at RT 2017 and talk over this story idea I had. Both times, I felt nervous about putting the Sweet Sixteen concept into words. Would they look at me in horror? Tell me this is about the least romantic idea they've ever heard?

They did not. Both of them were enthusiastic and supportive. And to get that kind of feedback from women I admire, well, that meant the world to me. Both of them had lots of people vying for their attention, but they both carved out some time for me. That meant a great deal.

I wouldn't have finished this book on time—or possibly at

all—without my beta reading team. Janett Gomez, Lisa Kuhne, Chelle Northcutt, Chantal Gemperle and Lizette Diaz—thank you. Thank you for reading the chapters fast when I was churning them out and waiting patiently when I wasn't. Chelle's messages about how she hated this book yet couldn't stop reading it were food for my artistic soul. And Lisa helped me with the blurb at a time when I needed her most. Janett's reactions to the pivotal chapters in the story encouraged me to write the ones after. You five gave me the fuel I needed to finish this story, just by reading it and cheering me on. So much love to you all.

Design Goddess Regina Wamba made the cover for Sweet Sixteen. With almost nothing to work with, she discovered my vision for this story. It wasn't quick or easy, but she didn't care about those things. She just wanted it to be perfect for me. The cover of this book is everything I hoped for and more.

Karen Hulseman read this story when it was being posted one chapter at a time on a startup reading app last year. It wasn't convenient and it left her hanging every time, but she did it, and she talked about the book, to support me. BIG HUGS, Karen.

My publicist Jessica Estep provided encouragement and organization when I needed them most. And Michelle New helped make my promo materials shine with her teaser wizardry.

Editors Lisa Hollett and Taylor Bellitto whipped this book into shape. They busted me on all my mistakes and helped me smooth out the rocky bits. Lisa also sat down with me at RT 2017 to discuss the book, and she helped me talk out my plot plan. And both Lisa and Taylor worked on my crazy schedule, which they may be used to doing but still puts them at rock star status for me.

My author bestie Stephanie Reid helped me with plotting on this book, providing a crucial turn that benefitted the story greatly. She is and always will be my plot whisperer.

My other author bestie Chelle Bliss formatted the book for me when I found myself in a time crunch. She's pretty much the best in every possible way.

And finally, thanks to Dan Hopkins for patiently answering all my football questions. There were many, and some were dumb, but he drew pictures when needed.

about the author

BRENDA ROTHERT LIVES IN CENTRAL Illinois. She was a daily print journalist for nine years, during which time she enjoyed writing a wide range of stories.

These days Brenda writes Contemporary Romance. She loves to hear from readers.

connect with Brenda

www.brendarothert.com

books by BRENDA ROTHERT

NOW SERIES

Now and Then

Now and Again

Now and Forever

FIRE ON ICE SERIES

Bound

Captive

Edge

Drive

Release

ON THE LINE SERIES

Killian

Bennett

LOCKHART BROTHERS SERIES

Deep Down

In Deep

Drawn Deeper

Hidden Depth

STANDALONES

Unspoken

Barely Breathing

Blown Away
Dirty Work (with Chelle Bliss)
Dirty Secret (with Chelle Bliss)
Dirty Defiance (with Chelle Bliss)
His
Hooked
Come Closer
Alpha Mail
Do You Like My Wiener